RUMBLE IN THE JUNGLE

Ranjit Lal has written over 35 books—fiction and non-fiction—for children and adults from 10 to 100 years old. His special interests include natural history, birds, dogs, photography, humour and automobiles. His book *Faces in the Water* won the Crossword-Vodafone award for Children's Writing for 2010 and the Ladli National Media Award for Gender Sensitivity for 2011-2012 and was honoured by IBBY. He lives in Delhi.

Published by Scholastic India Pvt. Ltd.
A subsidiary of Scholastic Inc., New York, 10012 (USA).
Publishers since 1920, with international operations in Canada, Australia, New Zealand, the United Kingdom, India, and Hong Kong.

ISBN-13: 978-93-5275-636-0

First edition: December 2018

This edition: February 2020

Printed in India at MicroPrints India, New Delhi

Rumble in the Jungle

RANJIT LAL

SCHOLASTIC
New York Toronto London Auckland
Sydney New Delhi Hong Kong

A MESSAGE FROM SCHOLASTIC INDIA

I love talking animals. From Lewis Carroll and Frank L Baum to Philip Pullman and JK Rowling, some of the best-loved books have had them.

This book not only has animals that talk, but also many other funny, brave and loyal characters. Full of adventure, drama, friendship and suspense, Ranjit Lal's singular ability to draw you into his worlds of wonder is unmatched, and I do hope you like it as much as I did.

Shantanu Duttagupta
Publisher

1

Prince Shamsher Bahadur Rana Thakursingh, the twelve-year-old scion of the ex-royal house of Gaindagunj, lay back on his cool silk pillows and smiled at his dadiji, sitting next to him on the bed.

'Dadi, tell me the story of Daduji's great rhino hunt again! You promised me you would!' he said. Now you might snort derisively and remark that a twelve-year-old should not be having bedtime stories told to him—what a wuss, but this was a 'first-night-at-home-for-the-holidays' ritual that the prince's grandmother had followed ever since he had been sent off to boarding school two years ago. And the young prince loved it. Ever since he could remember, he had loved hearing tales of the great rhino, tiger and elephant hunts of the past. How he had longed to be one of the great hunters, standing with his trusty rifle over his trophy, with a foot casually on its neck, and an admiring crowd around him. He would have, of course, taken down the great beast with a single shot even as it charged at him, head down or fangs bared, depending on what it was. He would modestly show these pictures to the boys at school ('Ya, boring really, but this is what I did in the holidays ...'), and dribbling with admiration, they would fight over who was to have the privilege of polishing his shoes. Even the teachers would nod respectfully at him. It really was such a pity that hunting had been banned— particularly in national parks such as Gaindagunj.

He hated boarding school. He'd quickly been nicknamed 'Prince Shame-Shame' by all the other crass boys because he had at first refused to use the common toilet and demanded a private one. Also, being skinny and pale, with huge dark eyes and long curling eyelashes (that some of his lady teachers swooned over), had not helped and he had been bullied incessantly. His father had churlishly insisted he stick it out as it would be 'a character-building experience'. (He'd had private tutors for his own education, though, of course, no one dared to point that out because he'd fly into a rage and throw cut-glass whisky decanters at the chandeliers.)

'Of course, darling, whatever you say,' the ex-maharani agreed, not really listening (she rarely did). She spent most of her time with her head in a cloud of expensive perfume, shopping in exclusive 'boutique shops' in Paris and Geneva, going on serial luxury cruises in the Mediterranean and hobnobbing with other socialites.

'Yes,' the ex-maharaja went on. 'It'll teach him to be a man. An alpha male like me! He's becoming a silly little girlie. You women have spoilt him sick here, coddling him and stuffing mithai into his mouth night and day.'

Which was exactly what the prince's dadiji had just done—partly because the maharaja and the maharani were currently rocking the casinos of Monte Carlo and would remain there for much of the summer. Now she soothed his brow, patted his cheeks and recounted the story yet again as the prince listened, entranced.

'... And so, there was your daduji, face to face with the most enormous, red-eyed, evil-tempered rhinoceros in the world, which was snorting and blowing smoke from its nostrils like your father's old Bugatti on a cold winter morning! That terrifying beast was at least twenty feet long and seven feet tall, and every time he stomped his great feet, the trees around him trembled and shook. He weighed at least ten tons and his great curved horn was six feet long! Your daduji had just one bullet left in his trusty Winchester ... Oh yes, he had fired many shots at the rhino, but the bullets had all bounced off the beast's armour like ping pong balls. Strewn around him lay the hunting party's fifty elephants, upside down in the mud, helplessly flapping their big ears and waving their stumpy legs and trunks in the air like capsized cockroaches. The great rhino had charged and butted them all, scornfully tossing them aside like ninepins—or rather elephant-pins! The Royal Hunting Party accompanying your daduji had all been thrown off and had scuttled away like beetles into the high grass, leaving your daduji all alone to face the great slavering monster.'

'Wow! Oh wow! What happened then?'

'You know, rhinos can't see very well—they have terrible myopia—and your daduji was a very fair man. So he tossed his reading glasses across to the rhino and snapped, "Wear them, then come at me! At least you'll see where I am and not blunder into another elephant!"'

'Wow!'

'Alas, the rhino just crushed the glasses to powder under his great feet. He didn't need them! You see rhinos have an excellent sense of smell and hearing; and your daduji was, I'm afraid, excessively fond of Killer Axeman aftershave and was reeking of it …' His dadiji sighed and fanned her face and murmured under her breath, 'Sometimes I think he sprayed it on to keep me away from him too—it made me nauseous, but may his soul rest in peace anyway!' She looked fondly at her grandson and went on, 'So the beast knew exactly where your daduji was! He just lowered his great head and charged. They say the nearest seismograph—you know, the machine that measures earthquakes—which was 400 km away, registered 8 on the Richter scale!'

'Dadiji ... no!' Prince Shammy's olive black eyes grew huge.

'Your daduji took aim ... and gently squeezed the trigger ...'

'And ... and ...? Did he get him?'

His dadiji lowered her voice and eyes. 'And the rifle jammed ...' she whispered. She smiled and nodded, her grey eyes twinkling. 'And now I think you should go to sleep ... I'll tell you the rest of the story tomorrow.'

'Dadiji, no! Tell me, tell me now!'

'Ah, all right then! So then your daduji cast his useless rifle aside and reached for the long throwing knife in his belt. His arm whipped back and he threw it with all his strength. It speared into the rhino's forehead, piercing the tough hide like a knife through hot butter, splicing the great rhino's brain clean into two. But the rhino was still thundering on at 50 kmph and your daduji deftly stepped aside only just in time. Then the great beast fell on its knees beside your daduji and died!'

'Wow!'

'And then all the holy men crawled out of the high grass and began the great tarpan ceremony. They dragged the great rhino to the banks of the bheel and cut it open. This ceremony was started many thousands of years ago, they say, by the Rajputs in Rajputana. And all the maharajas in our region had to do it once they ascended the throne, to appease the spirit of their ancestors. So they cut open the great beast and your daduji had to go inside its stomach and offer a palmful of its ruby blood to the gods, so that his papa's soul could rest in peace ...'

'Did it?'

His dadiji shrugged. 'Who knows, beta? Maybe, maybe not! But your daduji's spirit was certainly moved. He had to crawl inside the rhino's stomach, and when he came out and cleaned himself up, he told me, "Such a magnificent beast—it was like being inside a cathedral full of tomato puree! Whether Papaji is at peace or not, I will never know. All I know is that this great beast and his kind possesses courage, magnificence and grandeur that we can't even dream of—and we must honour that! A little, just a little of that courage seeped into me this evening." He had tears in his eyes. And then he decreed that the Royal Hunting Estate of Gaindagunj would become a sanctuary where rhinos would be protected forevermore. Later, the Government notified Gaindagunj as a national park and actually requisitioned the Palace's own Special Rhino Protection Group, the SRPG—set up and funded for eternity by Daduji—to provide armed security to the rhinos living there.'

'Dadiji, did Papa perform this ceremony after Daduji died?' the prince now asked.

His dadiji's eyes flashed. 'Oh yes, many people wanted him to, but I forbade him! Besides, your papa was too busy gambling and drinking in the casinos at Monte Carlo all the time … and anyhow, legally we were no longer royalty.' She looked fondly at her grandson. She had failed to bring up his father correctly—he was nothing but a playboy and wastrel, frittering away his legacy and chucking his weight around, throwing tantrums even a two-year-old would be ashamed of. The little prince would not follow his footsteps—she would see to it. He was lying back in bed now, a beatific expression on his beautiful face, his eyes gently closing.

Actually that was because the greatest idea of his life had just struck the prince like a god's thunderbolt. Fact: Papa's degenerate soul certainly needed saving! And now he knew just how to do it. And maybe then Papa would pull him out of his awful boarding school too. And he would save his papa's soul while he was still alive, not dead! That would be a bonus, surely! Also, once he did it, he the prince would be treated with a lot more respect at school (if he still had to go there, you never knew with Papa!) and all the other louts would have to bow before him and say 'Ji huzoor' to his every whim! Dare they call him Prince Shame-Shame ever again! Yes sir, he would do it!

It would take careful plotting—no one at the palace must be allowed to get a whiff of suspicion of what he was planning, not even Mutthiji who was his aide-de-camp, faithful bodyguard and companion, and a cousin of his father who had sworn to protect the prince and keep him from loneliness on account of his parents' perpetual absence. Yes, it would be betraying Mutthiji, but he had no choice. Mutthiji would throw a fit if he knew, and never allow it. And the deed had to be done before the holidays were over and he was dispatched back to school.

'Raja ...' his grandmother softly called, 'are you awake? Tomorrow I've arranged for you to go on safari in the jungle with Commander Thapa to see some of the rhinos at Akash bheel. His little daughter will be coming along too—she's a lovely girl and you can make friends with her.' She nodded to herself. Such a thing would be unheard of in the old days—a prince playing with the daughter of one of the palace's functionaries—but she had always been progressive in her outlook and cared two hoots about what the maharaja and maharani might think. Besides, the prince was all by himself here (Mutthiji notwithstanding) and that was not nice—he needed a friend or playmate of around his own age.

*

In a small clearing adjoining Akash bheel, an hour's elephant ride east of Gaindagunj Palace, Rumble-Tumble the rambunctious baby rhino none-too-gently nudged his mother's tummy.

'Go on, baba, you can't be hungry again!' she grunted fondly, moving away. 'You've just guzzled thirty litres straight off and haven't even burped!'

'Mamma, has my horn grown since this morning? I think it has! Has it? Will you measure it? Now! Measure it, measure it!'

'Yes, yes, I'm sure it has. Now go to sleep, baba! You know tomorrow is Masi's Day. In the evening, all your aunties and their babies will be coming to the bheel for the weekly swim and wallow …'

'Will Papa be coming too?'

His mother, the highly temperamental and redoubtable Gaindaben, snorted. 'Who knows what your papa wants? He just turns up when he feels like it and causes chaos. Butts around and upsets everybody.' Certainly old Hulla (short for Hullabaloo), Rumble-Tumble's rollicking old man, upset her. He threw his (considerable) weight around, flirted outrageously with all the other lady rhinos (and even wild boar and buffalo —like most rhinos he was short-sighted and sometimes they smelt very similar!) and then tried cuddling up to her—and she, despite her four-inch-thick armoured hide, fell for it every time! He could still turn her hefty rhino knees to jelly. That's what irritated the heck out of her. Her darling baba nudged her again.

'Mamma, tell me the story of Nanaji's great hunt … Tell me, tell me, tell me!'

'You've already heard it.'

'Again! I want to hear it again! Again, and again! Now!' Rumble-Tumble stomped his feet and butted his mother again. 'Now, now, now!'

'Oh … all right, you know, you really are becoming quite a spoilt brat!'

'Tell me the story, Mamma!'

'Uff baba, if you can be quiet for a moment and listen …' The hyper young rhino quietened down as his mother recounted the story.

'… And so, there was your nanaji, the greatest rhinoceros that ever lived, with his back to the bheel, where the maggarmachchs waited with their jaws agape, grinning evilly. Arrayed in a semi-circle in front of him were 500 war elephants in full body armour, with crossbow archers and gunners on their backs, their weapons primed and cocked. And in the lead was the maharaja, with a rocket-propelled grenade launcher on his shoulder.'

'But, isn't that unfair? One against so many, and with such big weapons?'

'That's how human beings are, baba … that's how they like to fight.'

'What happened then?'

'Your nanaji lowered his head and charged at the maharaja's elephant. The maharaja fired his grenade launcher, "phoom!" as did all the other marksmen their weapons. Such a terrible noise those Gatling guns made! So much fire and smoke! Still your nanaji thundered on. He would have tossed the maharaja's elephant—which had already turned tail to flee, and was trumpeting "bachao, bachao!"—into the bheel like flotsam and jetsam, and slashed the maharaja to ribbons with his incisors, but just then …'

The great rhino mom paused and shifted her bulk, swallowing.

Rumble-Tumble butted her none too gently. 'But just then what? Mamma, what happened? Tell me!'

His mother continued softly, 'Over the sound of all the firing and chaos came another terrible sound: the whup! whup! whup! of six Apache attack helicopter gunships bristling with laser guided Tomahawk missiles. They rose menacingly over the trees, glinting like evil metallic dragonflies, and swooped in. Your brave nanaji had no chance …' Rumble-Tumble's mom swallowed a lump and stomped her feet, annoyed that she was getting upset.

'And then?' Rumble-Tumble whispered, outraged.

'And then … and then …' his mom could barely go on, 'and then they all proclaimed that it was the maharaja's grenade launcher that killed your nanaji! That he had performed his sacred duty towards his ancestors! That their souls would find peace. Pah!'

She snorted again. 'It took them six months to decontaminate the bheel area—such was the firefight that evening. It also took that long before any plants dared to grow back. Fortunately, they seem to have given up the practice since then. Your nanaji may have died, but he taught them a lesson they haven't forgotten.'

'And this happened at the bheel?'

'Yes, here at Akash bheel, no less! Where we go swimming and wallowing ... where you'll meet your aunties and their babies tomorrow as usual.'

Rumble-Tumble squinted. How he would have loved to have been his nanaji. To charge a battalion of 500 war elephants bristling with marksmen! He would have knocked them flat, no problem! He would have brought down those helicopters too. He would have stomped the stupid maharaja to pulp!

And that would show that toffee-nosed Roly-Poly who thought she was so superior to them all and such a VILR (Very Important Little Rhino). He gulped.

'Mamma,' he asked shyly, 'will Roly-Poly be coming down to the bheel tomorrow?'

His mom snorted. 'I don't know. But I've told you to stay away from her. She's not one of us anymore! That girl has no shame! No dignity!'

'So who wants to be friends with her?' he protested, trying to sound disgusted. 'I just thought it might be fun to biff her roly-poly butt into the bheel where Smiley Masi can snap her jaws at her and give her a fright. That'll teach her to strut around with her snout in the air!' His mother squinted at him fondly. How could anyone be angry at him for more than two minutes tops? Such a golu-molu plump darling he was! She smiled indulgently and nudged him … and winked.

'Baba, there are so many other little girl rhinos you can tease and chase instead. But don't butt them into the bheel—their mothers don't have a sense of humour and won't see the funny side. And you know, Smiley Masi is not to be trusted—she might just decide that one of the baby rhinos is a sausage roll after all, and then you'll be in trouble with the mothers and the SRPG.'

Even so, Rumble-Tumble hoped that Roly-Poly would be at the bheel the following evening. He stomped his feet. Sure there would be many baby rhinos around tomorrow to play with, bully and toss around, but he wasn't too interested in them. Most of them went bawling to their mammas when he playfully butted them and then his mother got upset and would ground him and forbid him from playing in the mud. But yes, he wanted to impress Roly-Poly, no question about that: and not only because she was one snooty little prima-donna who trotted around tossing her little stumpy head in the air. She really had very cute, wiggly ears. He snorted again and suddenly pricked up his own ears: something large, very large, was blundering through the high grass, and approaching them. His mother too flicked her ears and shifted her great bulk, snorting warningly. The park's twelve tigers wouldn't dare attack a full-grown rhino, but they couldn't be trusted about not trying to snatch a baby.

'Who goes there?' Gaindaben snorted. 'Identify yourself or I will charge! First, last and final warning!'

'Cool your jets, Gaindaben, it is me, Bhaisaraja …'

An enormous wild water buffalo with an eight-foot horn-span materialized out of the grass, the silver moonlight glinting off his polished granite back. His jaws moved languidly from side to side and round and round as he chewed his (gutka actually—but don't tell anyone) cud.

'What do you want, Bhaisa? Not more grazing rights!' Gaindaben snorted.

'Of course not, behenji … I bring glad tidings. The royal prince, His Highness Shamsher Bahadur Rana Thakursinghji Blah Blah Blah, has arrived at the palace and will be spending his holidays here. Do inform the other ladies so that from tomorrow they ensure that the prince gets good views of them and their babies when he comes on safari.'

'We are not zoo animals on display!' Gaindaben snorted. 'If they want to admire our great bulk and sleek beauty, they must seek us out. But yes, tomorrow is Masi's Day at the bheel and we should all be there. The SRPG know that …'

'So make sure you do your toilette, eh? Powder your faces and whatnot and whatever else you ladies do with the mud …'

'Pah!'

And then, Rumble-Tumble's little eyes gleamed as an idea went click, click, click in his stumpy little head.

*

'Giddy-up, giddy-up, giddy-up girl, that's the way to go, Roly-Poly, yoohoo!' Snub-nosed, tousled-haired Teesta, all of nine years old, sat bareback astride the bouncing baby rhino as she careened around the paddock, snorting happily. The little girl's eyes, black as a carpenter bee, shone with mischief and delight. She knew what she was doing was highly illegal, but she also knew that her father, Commander Bahadur Thapa, the leader of the SRPG, and mother had gone to the palace to pay their respects to the prince who had just arrived for his holidays. They would not be back for a couple of hours at least. Well, they weren't her real parents, of course, because she had been adopted after her real parents had been killed by a gang of drunken wild elephants when she was a tiny baby, but sometimes she thought they were better than real parents (judging by what some of her school friends said about their real parents.) Most of the other members of the SRPG, who also treated her like she was their own little girl, were now out on patrol on their elephants, and anyway, their living quarters were a little distance away. Commander Thapa had left Roly-Poly safe and comfortable in her stable, its heavy doors bolted.

'Rani, now you be a good girl and go to sleep; we'll be back by ten,' her mother had told Teesta, adjusting her pallu and checking her face in the hall mirror. Her father looked dashingly handsome in his black uniform as he stood to attention, sub-machine gun across his chest, finger on trigger (this pose had become a habit with him) beside his Gypsy.

'Yes, Mamma,' Teesta had replied innocently. She had waited for ten minutes, then hopped out of bed and simply led the baby rhino through the corridor linking the stable to the kitchen and dining room, out of the front door of the house and into the paddock.

Teesta was slim, brown and winsome. One moment she could be fidgety and jumpy as a whirligig beetle on a sugar high, the next, calm and soothing as a slow loris doing yoga. She would never forget that traumatic evening, nearly three months ago, which had turned her life upside down, and even now could not understand exactly what had happened.

Teesta attended the Gaindagunj National Park High School located just across the Gaindagunj river, which flowed along the southern boundary of the national park. She was dropped and picked up from school on cycle by one of the SRPG men, usually Jawahar Singh, who was her favourite because he had so many stories to tell. On that fateful afternoon, Jawahar Singh had failed to turn up and, impatient as ever, Teesta had decided to walk home on her own—not a sensible decision as she would have to walk through rutted jungle tracks inside the park, which was forbidden. En route, she had been alerted by the faint distress bleats of an animal and had decided to investigate, plunging deeper into the jungle. And, suddenly, she had found herself falling headlong into a pit dug by poachers which had just claimed the life of an enormous female rhino called Lilabai. The bleating came from her dazed baby, still trying to suckle from her dead mother. Teesta and the baby rhino (who she named Roly-Poly) stayed in the pit all night. The little girl sang to the terrified little animal to soothe it (and calm herself). Fortunately they were found early next morning, as was Jawahar Singh, who was lying out cold nearby after having been attacked by the poachers.

She was almost unconscious when found, having spent a wet night in the pit, perched on the flanks of the dead rhino, holding a seemingly dead baby rhino's head in her lap. As water had started collecting in the pit,

Teesta had clambered onto the mother rhino, somehow hoisting the semi-conscious baby up with her, so that at least its head remained above water and cradled in her lap. She was crinkly wet, shivering with cold and blotched with insect bites, but her arms around the baby rhino's head were vice-like and would not let go. The baby rhino was barely alive.

They took them both to the SRPG's headquarters (and where Teesta lived), informing the park authorities to send over a doctor and a vet. Thankfully, all was well. Though the baby rhino was still very weak, with care and medication she would surely get better. But yes, one more rhino had been poached and that was a very bad thing indeed.

Teesta spent just a single day in bed. She was a tough little cookie who had no patience with germs. Neither of her parents had taken her to task for breaking the rules. They had simply looked at her as she lay in bed, pale and drawn, not quite looking them in the eye. They knew that she had realized what she had done—and had been punished enough, and would never do anything so silly again. But she had, hopefully, saved the life of a baby rhino, no question about that. All too soon, the mischief was back in her bright eyes.

Early the following morning, before the household had awoken, Teesta had hopped out of bed and made her way to the stable where the baby rhino had been kept.

The little animal lay on her side, a roly-poly traumatized little thing, breathing heavily and refusing the milk she was being offered.

'She'll die if she doesn't drink it,' one of the guards told Teesta, holding up a bottle of warm, sweet milk. 'We can't give her an IV drip forever.' She had taken the bottle from him and gone up to the uncaring little rhino, cowering in a corner, too weak now to even attempt to charge.

'Roly-Poly! That's what I'm going to call you. Now drink up your milk—it's good for you. I'm sorry about your mamma. We'll find the rascals who killed her and then you can butt their bottoms good and proper.'

The little rhino had opened her eyes and gazed short-sightedly at Teesta's tousled nut brown face and sparkling eyes. She sniffed the air and flicked her ears. She knew that voice and smell—they were comforting, soothing and kind and she had missed them. Teesta thrust the feeding bottle into her mouth.

'There you go, baby—now drink it up.'

And then the little rhino had thrust her snout at the bottle and guzzled its entire contents as Teesta's eyes grew wide with delight. The guards could only mutter, 'Wah wah!' in amazement.

After that, the baby rhino and Teesta were virtually inseparable. The pudgy little baby would follow Teeta around everywhere in the house and outside, snorting and nudging and butting her gently to draw attention, and throw a tantrum when the little girl had to leave for school. She had even bashed right through the bathroom door once! Jawahar Singh, who had recovered from his injuries (he was a tough old bird), cleverly introduced a yellow-eyed sardonic old billy goat called Bakrasahib as a companion for the little rhino for when Teesta was at school. Of course, the moment she returned, Roly-Poly would make her preference quite clear, and Bakrasahib would snort contemptuously and wag his beard, as if to say, 'Pah! Little girl rhinos are so silly and fickle, it's unbelievable!'

It was Teesta who fed her: milk from a bottle, mashed bananas, carrots, cauliflower, grass and hay. She took her out to the elephants' large paddock (where she was now cavorting) for exercise and fresh air. Once Roly-Poly had settled down, they had started taking her out into the jungle—all the way to Akash bheel—in an attempt to introduce her to what would hopefully one day become her home. The little rhino had kept close to Teesta and the elephants, who escorted her protectively and had quietly stared at Gaindaben and Rumble-Tumble who had stared back at her amazed. Then, Gaindaben had emitted a contemptuous snort and turned on her heel and rolled away, but Rumble-Tumble had followed his mother reluctantly, pausing every now and then to look back at her, his ears flicking this way and that. Roly-

Poly had tossed her little head up and snorted equally derisively, as Teesta looked on, thrilled to bits.

'I think he likes you!' she whispered. 'Really Roly-Poly, you work fast! You've already got a boyfriend!'

To her utter amazement, the little rhino had not objected at all when she had, one quiet afternoon not long ago, daringly climbed onto her back, and had ridden her around the paddock, a grin as wide as the Brahmaputra river stretched across her face. Her mother had nearly freaked out.

'Rani, get off her at once. She's a wild rhinoceros, not a tattu pony! She'll toss you and trample you! What are you thinking?' She turned to her husband, who was trying to hide an admiring smile. 'And what will people think? My daughter riding a rhinoceros! It is not ladylike at all. Like ladies wearing shorts and riding motorcycles and what have you.'

'And she's riding bareback too. Just look at her!'

'Really, ji, you are as bad as her!'

'She likes it, Mamma,' Teesta had replied naughtily, but had been quickly ordered down.

'Giddy-up!' she yelled again now as Roly-Poly huffed and puffed around the paddock like a little steam engine with Teesta perched perkily on her back. Jawahar Singh emerged from his room and walked up to the paddock, a broad smile on his face.

'Baby, maar padegi—you'll get into trouble. Get down! Mummy-papa gussa honge—your mummy and papa will be angry!'

'Hah—if the Rani of Jhansi could ride a horse, why can't I ride a rhino?'

Jawahar Singh had no answer to that and could only grin.

'Sambhalna—be careful!' he said, squatting down to watch. It was astonishing how the little girl and baby rhino had bonded. Well, maybe it was expected after Teesta had spent an entire night cuddling her, telling her stories and singing to her as the rain came down. The baby rhino had probably forgotten its real mother and thought of Teesta as her mom.

'Teesta baby, we'll take her out to the bheel again tomorrow,' he said. 'The rajkumar has come and will be going there to see the wildlife.'

Teesta slipped off Roly-Poly and put her arm around the rhino's fat neck and made a face.

'Maybe I can get Roly-Poly to charge him! That'll show him!'

Jawahar Singh stood up, grinning. 'Okay,' he said, 'but I think you should go back inside now—and take her to her stable. I can see the headlights of your papa's Gypsy approach.'

Tucked up innocently in bed, Teesta pretended to open a sleepy eye as her mother stepped into her room to check on her. She came in and sat at her bedside.

'Teesta?' she called softly.

'Mmm … Mamma?' Teesta pretended to yawn, and turned over.

'Rani, you've been riding that rhino again, haven't you?'

'What? Mamma … I'm sleepy …'

'I'm sure you are. Both of you have left footprints all over the kitchen and dining room floor.'

'Oh shoot, I knew I forgot something!' Teesta said involuntarily, and then quickly shut her eyes.

'Yes, you did. And you know you shouldn't do that. It's not proper for a young girl to ride on a rhino—what will the rajkumar or rajmataji think if they knew? Now baby, the rajkumar's dadiji has invited you to the palace tomorrow afternoon. You will later accompany Rajkumar Shamsher on safari in the jungle with Papa on Maharani … The rajkumar's come home for the holidays.'

'But Mamma, what about Roly-Poly? I can't ditch her. We were going to take her to the bheel tomorrow.'

'She'll be all right. Maybe you can still take her along with you—you should be passing by when you're on your way to the bheel and can pick her up then.'

'Mamma, do I have to? He's a snotty-nosed …'

'Baby, his dadiji said he's very lonely and has no one to play with.'

Teesta opened her dark eyes, a small wicked smile lighting up her face. 'Yeah, maybe I can teach him to ride Roly-Poly! I bet he'll chicken out,' she said, watching her mother's horrified face. 'Just joking, Mamma,' she giggled. 'Just joking! I'll be good.'

Her mother kissed her and left the room. She was not quite sure that her daughter had indeed been joking. There had been a gleam in the little girl's eye that had indicated something quite different.

2

'Beta, the little girl has arrived and is waiting in the Durbar Hall downstairs. Come along and meet her.' Prince Shamsher's dadiji pushed open the door to the prince's bedroom that afternoon and entered. Her hand flew up to her mouth and she hid a smile. Prince Shamsher Rana Thakursinghji was preening in front of a full-length mirror. He was dressed in long khaki shorts, a khaki shirt with epaulettes, which were crisscrossed with leather bandoliers across his skinny chest, and a sola topee. He was holding a 0.22 Daisy airgun in his hand.

'Beta, why are you dressed like Jim Corbett?' his dadiji asked.

'Because we're going into the jungle on safari and I always dress like this when we do that. Dadiji, how do I look?'

'Very dashing—I'm sure the little girl will be very impressed. But you don't need the gun—Commander Thapa and his men will be carrying guns as usual.'

'This little girl—she's Commander Thapa's daughter?'

'Yes, and she is a very brave little girl too! She once spent the entire night in a ditch in the rain cradling a baby rhino in her lap and singing lullabies to it, waiting for rescue.'

'Hah! But she's just nine and I'm twelve! We live on different planets.'

He followed Dadiji down the sweeping marble staircase to the great Durbar Hall. Ornate gold-painted mahogany chairs with fussily carved legs upholstered in maroon velvet lined the walls of the great wood-panelled room. Its wooden floor gleamed with polish. Huge slightly musty chandeliers rocked gently on their moorings from the ceiling, and the heads of tigers, leopards, wild buffalo, sambar, nilgai, and yes, even rhino, looked down at them from the walls—trophies of past hunts. At one end of the room, four huge tiger skins sprawled on the floor, surrounded by plush sofas and settees.

Prince Shammy looked around, and then spotted the little girl, sitting primly on one of the chairs against the wall. She was wearing tough-looking dungarees over an olive shirt and fiddled with a beige baseball cap in her hands. Her eyes were black and bright, and she had tied her hair back in a perky ponytail. She stood up and came forward as the prince and his grandmother approached her. Outside, in the forecourt, he could see a couple of elephants waiting. Dadiji smiled and made the introductions.

'Beta, this is Teesta, whom I told you about. Teesta, dear, this is Prince Shamsher.'

Teesta smiled, perking up an eyebrow. 'Hi, can I call you Shammy?' she asked brightly, and not in the least intimidated.

'What?' He was taken aback. He was sure the little girl would bow, or curtsy, or try and touch his feet as most village children did—not ask him if she could call him 'Shammy'. He shrugged, trying to be nonchalant.

'I guess, if you want!' He could think of nothing rude he could say in return.

'You're dressed like an Angrezi murgi-shikari,' she pointed out, not in the least shy. 'Why?'

'Uh-huh—we're going into the jungle after all …'

'Hmm … you like living surrounded by dead animals?' she asked, pointing to the 'trophies' lining the walls.

'I didn't kill them,' he said defensively, though secretly he wished he had. 'They were shot years and years and years ago by my ancestors.'

'Ya, maybe you should take them down and put them away. They give me the creeps. How would you like it if someone shot you and put your head on a wall for hundreds of years?' She giggled. 'Though, then of course you'd be able to hear what people said about you.'

He glared at her balefully. Was she trying to be funny or what? Well, she was just nine years old, so what could you expect?

'Come on, let's go. Papa's waiting outside on Maharani.'

'Good, you two have made friends so quickly,' Dadiji gushed, patting them both on the head. 'Now you go and have a good time. Beta, have you taken your binoculars and water bottle?'

'Yes, Dadiji. I gave them to Mutthiji. He's outside.'

Mutthiji, of course, would accompany the prince —he went everywhere with him. He was most un-bodyguard like: fair, rotund and balding, with shrewd, bulging eyes and soft pudgy hands. But it was rumoured he was a crack shot and could take out the eye of a sunbird at 500 yards with a single shot, and was really very strong. He had a petulant high-pitched, squeaky voice that had made gruffer-voiced men laugh at him all his life. He was now standing beside Commander Thapa and Maharani, who swayed and mused, shifting from one pillar-like leg to another.

The children went down and approached the elephant, the prince, a trifle nervously.

'Maharani oopar!' Teesta barked, and the huge beast gently curled her trunk around her waist and lifted her up onto her broad back, depositing her behind her mahout, Madhav Rao.

Prince Shammy went pale. Oh god, was this gigantic monster going to lift him up the same way? But Madhav Rao had started guiding the elephant towards the special raised platform that had been built for royalty to climb on and get off elephants' backs without losing their dignity, rather like an airplane's staircase.

'Beta, you climb on from here,' Commander Thapa told the rather relieved prince.

'Now come along—we'll show you how the rhinos here are protected.'

Teesta giggled. 'It's just like the way those fat netas are guarded. Each rhino has one or two stern guards in black uniforms wearing bandanas shadowing it, guns ready to fire! We'll go to the bheel now—they love wallowing there ...'

They set off, eastwards towards the bheel, watching chital, sambar and wild boar rootling about in the tangled bushes, tall grass and undergrowth on the way. They passed the SRPG headquarters en route, where they were met by Jawahar Singh on his elephant Hira, and of course, Roly-Poly. The little rhino squealed with delight and ran round and round Maharani—who was getting a little jumpy with this pesky little heavyweight running in circles around her—as Teesta called out to her from her back.

'She's like a little pet dog,' Teesta told Prince Shammy proudly. 'She follows me around everywhere. She'll come after us now, all the way to the bheel.' They were soon joined by two more SRPG elephants.

'Her mother was poached from right under our noses,' Commander Thapa told the prince grimly. 'But we'll get the poachers sooner or later ... the thing is they must not take another rhino.'

They approached the bheel carefully, with little Roly-Poly safely sandwiched between the great legs of Maharani and Hira.

'Look!' Teesta pointed towards the bheel, where a giant rhino and its baby were galumphing in the mud. 'Isn't that Roly-Poly's boyfriend?'

*

Rumble-Tumble rolled over onto his feet, trying not to slip again in the gooey slick mud. He peered short-sightedly at the bank and could just about make out the looming bulk of the two big riding elephants. Ah, so they had come to 'view' them, as Bhaisaraja had said. Now he'd give the prince something to remember: he'd charge! But then, there was that unique perfume being borne on the breeze, accompanied by that squeal—they could only belong to one little rhino! The little prima donna was back. She was squealing away somewhere near the elephants. He waded manfully out of the pool as his mother watched him warily. He stood still, his ears flicking this way and that, his nostrils quivering.

Ah, yes, no doubt about it—she was back! There she was, that cute tubby little thing standing beside that elephant and looking his way. He stomped his feet and grunted. She tossed her stumpy little horn and did the same. He took a couple of steps forward. She ducked her head and bounced a little towards him.

'Look at her!' Teesta whispered. 'She's flirting with him.'

'Keep an eye on his mother,' her father warned. 'She may not approve, and charge.'

In the water, Gaindaben looked around myopically for her son.

'Rumble-Tumble, where are you, baba?' she called anxiously. Then she heard him stomp and grunt, and waded out of the water after him. There he was on the path, facing the two riding elephants—and that baby rhino who had shamed them all.

'Baba, I told you not to play with her! Why don't you listen to me? She's no good.'

'Mamma, it's okay, I'm just going to …' and with that, Rumble-Tumble lowered his head and charged towards the little rhino that was stomping and tossing her head in front of him.

'Roly-Poly, watch out!' Teesta screamed as Prince Shammy went pale. Commander Thapa watched tensely, and prepared to fire a shot in the air if the baby rhino's mother charged. But Roly-Poly just stamped her feet impatiently, snorted and waited.

Rumble-Tumble galloped towards her, grunting. She waited till he was nearly on her and then daintily skipped to one side, tossing her little head contemptuously in the air. Rumble-Tumble, who had only meant to gently nudge her, tripped over a log lying on the ground just behind her, rolled over and over right down the slope and into the bheel. He landed with an almighty splash that rudely woke up Smiley Masi who had been dozing in the shallows with her mouth wide open. She awoke with a mighty roar and snapped her great jaws ... and then saw the tubby rhino floundering in the water.

Silently, she submarined. One rhino sausage roll coming up!

'Papa, the croc's seen him,' Teesta cried. 'It's after him!'

Prince Shammy's mouth had fallen open as he watched the unfolding drama.

'Beta? Beta? Where are you?' Gaindaben looked around uncertainly. She had heard the commotion and the splash but had no idea who had fallen into the water. 'Heck, I really must get my eyes checked,' she muttered as she looked from side to side.

Roly-Poly stopped pirouetting and snorting, and suddenly stood very still. She had heard the splash and then there was silence. Where had the little bugger gone? She bounced towards the edge of the bank—oh no, had the little idiot fallen into the water?

'Have you fallen into the water?' she screamed. 'Get out, get out!' she stomped her feet and snorted.

Gaindaben swivelled around. Had that nasty little rhino shoved her beloved dumpling into the water? It seemed so. She snorted mightily and charged. Roly-Poly felt the earth tremble as the enraged rhino-mom barrelled towards her. She turned around to face her. Again, she dodged it at the last possible moment—she'd got good practice dodging Bakrasahib's mock charges.

And two tons of enraged rhino-mom flew over the bank of the bheel and landed with a report like a cannon, right on the back of Smiley Masi who had just begun to surface and whose back has never been the same since.

The tidal wave caused by Gaindaben's landing carried Rumble-Tumble towards the bank and he scrambled ashore, slipping and sliding in the slick mud. Roly-Poly trotted up and helped him scramble to safety by nudging and butting him along.

'You okay? You really shouldn't go swimming with crocodiles,' she said severely. 'It's stupid!'

'You … you …' he snorted, outraged, and then looked at her. Oh god, up close she was prettier than ever, the prettiest, cutest baby rhino he had ever set his eyes on, certainly. She even smelt pretty!

'Me … me … what?' she asked, nudging him again. 'Want to play tag?' she invited. She pirouetted as delicately as only a baby rhino can, and trotted off, tossing her head in the air. 'Catch me if you can!'

He blundered after her, suddenly very happy indeed.

His mother hauled herself out of the bheel and looked around. Where the hell had her ladla beta gone? Ah, there he was, running full pelt after that pesky little girl again.

'My mamma won't allow me to chase you,' Rumble-Tumble snorted.

'Then why are you chasing me?' Roly-Poly giggled.

'You wanted to play tag …'

'By the way, why did you charge at me?'

'Me? Charge at you? I didn't!'

'Did too … then I dodged you, and you fell into the water and nearly into that crocodile's mouth.'

'Did not! I just wanted to … to … say hello …'

Roly-Poly skidded to a halt. 'Well, hello then.'

'Hello to you too!' He lumbered to a halt beside her. They were now hidden from Gaindaben by the high grass, though up on Maharani's back, Teesta, her eyes wide like flying saucers, and Prince Shammy could see everything.

'Look at them!' Teesta whispered. 'They're romancing. At their age!'

Prince Shammy turned pink and Commander Thapa hid a grin.

The two baby rhinos were standing side by side, nudging each other.

'If my mom sees us like this, she'll feed me to Smiley Masi,' Rumble-Tumble said sadly. 'Where's your mom, by the way? I didn't see her …'

Roly-Poly looked puzzled. 'I don't really remember having a mom like yours—only that little girl … when I opened my eyes we were in this dark, wet, muddy place and I was very scared. She told me stories and sang sweetly to me … and now she rides me and we have fun, and there's Bakrasahib who I like to chase and …'

There was a sudden commotion and the two little rhinos stepped out of cover and looked around to see what was going on. Another rhino had appeared towards the far end of the bheel; a gargantuan fellow, tossing his mighty horn around, rolling up and down and doing doughnuts in the dust and grunting. Behind him, two SRPG guards on yet another elephant watched him warily.

Up on Maharani, Commander Thapa pointed and said, 'Look, old Hulla's come down to stir things up a bit.'

By now, there were half a dozen lady rhinos, some with their babies, around the bheel, and they all looked warily at the gigantic old fellow kicking up dust and showing off handbrake turns. Rumble-Tumble nudged Roly-Poly again.

'That's Papa!'

'Such a show-off, that fellow,' Teesta snorted. 'Look at him!'

The ladies with babies were hastily moving away into the high grass, urging their little ones ahead of them. Gaindaben peered at Hullabaloo and snorted.

'Oh, so you've turned up again. Before you do or say anything, no, I don't want to go out with you right now — or ever,' she said, which really was a lie. 'Besides, have you seen your son? Already chasing the wrong kind of girls! The most undesirable ones at that. Minnuben has had such a sweet little daughter, but will he look at her? No. He goes after that tomboy who's being raised by that hellion little girl and a buddha billy goat of all things! You know what she's going to turn out like. He's got all your bad habits.'

'Not my problem, babe!' Hulla snorted. 'Now, come on, it's a lovely morning for a walk, just me and you, and you don't want to upset me by saying no.'

'Hulla, go jump into the bheel and cool off, will you!'

'I'll cool you off right now. That's no way to speak to your lord and master!'

The huge rhino pawed the ground and lowered his head.

'Lord and master? More buffoon and bum!'

'I'll buffoon you here and now. Buffoon, buffoon, buffoon, here I come!'

Up on Maharani who was flapping her ears languidly, Teesta clutched her father's hand.

'Papa, he's going to charge her!'

The prince watched open-mouthed. So much was happening here, he barely knew where to look. But an idea was glimmering … yes … yes …

'He's just throwing his weight around as usual,' Commander Thapa said. 'I don't think he'll hurt her. He's just bluffing.'

Finally, it was the formidable Gaindaben who lost her patience, lowered her head and charged. She came up so fast and thunderous that the big buffoon rhino turned tail and crashed into the grass, backfiring like a badly-tuned old motorcycle, as his big behind got royally butted.

Gaindaben skidded to a halt, grunting in disgust as Hulla crashed away. 'Oh my god, oof, you nearly gassed me! What the heck do you eat? Half a ton of channe ka dal and rajma by the sound and smell of it!'

'That's showing him, Gaindaben!' Teesta crowed, exchanging high fives with the surprised prince. 'That's showing him!'

'Wow, I shouldn't get in the way of your mom,' Roly-Poly told Rumble-Tumble seriously, flicking her little ears. 'She's like a JCB on a rampage!'

'Mom has a few anger management issues when it comes to Papa,' Rumble-Tumble admitted. 'She says she might go for counselling—apparently there's this cow, Sidhvi Gaumataji, in the adjoining village who spent years doing yoga in the middle of some crazy town called Kolkata before retiring, and knows how to calm you down regardless of what's going on around you.'

'Heck, she's coming this way. She knows where we are. Gotta go … see you sometime, kiddo, nice meeting you.' Roly-Poly trotted off hastily towards where Maharani and the other elephants were calmly eating grass and swaying in their usual comfortable way, like ships at anchor.

'Baba, there you are! How many times have I told you not to play with that floozy? She lives with humans. God knows how many of their foul diseases and bad habits she carries. As it is, she nearly lured you into Smiley Masi's mouth. You'll be in deep water the next time I catch you with her, young man. Do you understand? Now come on and bathe properly in the bheel. I don't think Smiley Masi will bother us.'

'Yes, Mamma … Mamma, I'm thirsty. Can I have a milkshake?'

*

'Wow! Did you see that?' Teesta nudged the prince who was still looking a bit dazed. 'She just chased him away.

And look, Roly-Poly's back here with us ... Hey baby, it's all right. I'm up here!' Teesta would have dearly liked to slither down Maharani's trunk and be with Roly-Poly, but no chance of that happening. Not with her father around as well as so many rhinos.

'That fellow she chased away, is he the local goonda rhino?' Prince Shammy asked Commander Thapa. The commander nodded.

'Well, you could say so. We call him Hullabaloo, Hulla for short, because he always causes trouble wherever he goes. He loves raiding the villagers' fields and chasing calves, so they don't like him very much, and he comes here to upset and flirt with all the lady rhinos regardless of whether they have babies to look after or not. You saw him ... We try to have one elephant and two guards follow him 24 x 7 to ensure he stays out of trouble. He's a prime target for poachers because of his magnificent horn. I think they were after him but they caught Roly-Poly's mother instead.'

'Um ... where did you find Roly-Poly?' the prince asked.

'Come along, we'll show you ...' the commander said. 'Besides, I want to check that they've filled up the trap properly.'

Both Teesta and Roly-Poly quieted down as they approached the site. Teesta remembered the terrifying night she had spent with the little rhino and Roly-Poly experienced strange stirrings she could not understand

and kept close to the elephants who seemed to sense her distress. Maharani, gracious and sagacious as ever, nuzzled her comfortingly with her trunk.

The terrible ditch had been covered up properly.

'Uncle, how did the poachers know that rhinos came this way?' the prince asked, as they stared at the spot.

'Beta, we found a rhino latrine a little way up ahead – they do potty in the same place to mark their territory. So the poachers knew that and guessed that the rhino would have to come this way to get to the spot. It was, in fact, the only way they could have come. So they dug the trap here.'

'They might do it again.'

'Yes, but we check it – and other such spots – nearly every day. We have a Rhino Potty Plot map in the office, with all the sites we know of flagged.'

'Wow! I would like to see that.'

'Certainly, beta … anytime.'

They made their way back to the SRPG headquarters, where Teesta got off, and was greeted with a squeal of delight by Roly-Poly.

'Come down and meet her,' she called up to the prince. 'Make friends with her.' And before the prince knew what was happening, Maharani had curled her trunk around him, and deposited him lightly as a feather beside Teesta.

'Oh wow!'

Roly-Poly alas was not as gentle, and nudged him so hard that he fell over.

'Roly-Poly, be polite now. It's not nice to knock over your guest,' Teesta scolded, giggling. 'Are you okay?'

'Yes, yes, I'm fine!' The prince scrambled to his feet and looked at Roly-Poly. Really, he had to admit, she was cute and pudgy even if she didn't know her own strength. And that big fellow, Hullabaloo, had been truly magnificent; bigger than a Humvee.

'Chalo beta, I'll drop you home now,' the commander said, 'or your dadiji will start to worry.' Once again, Maharani hoisted him up onto her back.

'Uncle,' he asked the commander as they went on their way, 'do you know where that big fellow, Hullabaloo, goes to poop?'

Slowly, the prince's head was clearing.

'I'll have to check the map and see if we've marked the location,' the commander said. 'You've really taken a shine to him, haven't you?'

3

Teesta's holidays had also begun and she had planned (with her father, of course,) to take Roly-Poly out into the forest as much as she could so that the little rhino could start to feel at home in what really was her home. Akash bheel was a good place to go to because there were usually some rhinos there, feeding, grazing or wallowing. Gradually, Roly-Poly would get accustomed to her own kind—she was a friendly little soul and had already made friends with that ruffian little boy rhino. So Teesta and Commander Thapa were quite optimistic about re-introducing her back into the wild when she was old enough to look after herself. But they hadn't quite expected the message that came from Gaindagunj Palace later that evening after the first memorable safari to the bheel.

A liveried functionary from the palace, in gold braid and maroon and purple silk, had driven up in a Land Rover and had presented on a silver tray a gilt-edged card addressed to *Miss Teesta Thapa* in twirly typeface:

His Royal Highness, Rajkumar Shamsher Bahadur Rana Thakursinghji would request the pleasure of the company of Miss Teesta Thapa and Baby Rhino Roly-Poly at the Gaindagunj Palace tomorrow between 10 a.m. and 6 p.m.

RSVP

Teesta's mother was over the moon when she saw the invite. 'You've really been a good girl,' she said, hugging Teesta. 'You've made a good impression on the rajkumar. He wants you to spend the day with him at the palace! I'm so proud of you.'

'Mamma, he's just a boy like all other boys—snot-nosed like they all are,' Teesta remarked turning the card over and frowning. 'What does RSVP mean?'

'It means you have to reply to him. Of course you'll be going. The question is, what will you wear? All your normal clothes are rough-tough jungle clothes!'

'And what will Roly-Poly wear?' Teesta asked innocently. 'She's been invited too!' She frowned again. 'You know, Papa and I wanted to take Roly-Poly to the forest again from tomorrow ...'

'Rani, you've got so many more holidays. Spending one day at the palace won't make a difference.'

'Mamma,' Teesta said seriously, 'if Roly-Poly spends one day at Gaindagunj Palace, she may *never* want to go back to the jungle again!'

Her mother looked at her sardonically. 'Rani, after Roly-Poly spends one day at Gaindagunj Palace, the rajkumar may never want to invite you and her there again ...' she said and then hugged her daughter. 'But I suppose we have to obey his decree, so Roly-Poly must go.'

'Of course, Mamma!'

'Fine by me,' said Commander Thapa. 'Actually, it suits me well. I wanted to take Jawahar Singh and Hira on patrol tomorrow. We may have a lead regarding those poachers who killed Roly-Poly's mother. We'll drop you both at the palace in the morning and pick you up in the evening.'

'Papa, it's going to be so boring,' Teesta grumbled. Her father leaned over and whispered in her ear.

'Can you imagine what fun you can have with Roly-Poly running amok in the palace?' he whispered. Teesta giggled as her mother looked at them suspiciously.

'What?' she said. 'What did you tell her, ji? I know that look on your face!'

'Nothing, Mamma,' Teesta said innocently, and added seriously, 'In my RSVP I must tell Shammy to take down all those rhino and other animals' heads that are up on the walls. They might upset Roly-Poly.'

'Shammy? Who's that?'

'Oh, that prince fellow. He doesn't mind.'

So the following morning, Teesta, up on Maharani, rode royally up the palace's driveway, with Jawahar Singh following on Hira and Roly-Poly trotting between the two elephants. They reached sharp at 10 a.m. and there at the top of the marble steps, Prince Shamsher waited for them, dressed again like an 'Angrezi murgi-shikari'. His dadiji stood beside him, smiling.

'Hello, my dear!' she said. 'That must be Roly-Poly …'

Roly-Poly had just discovered a rose-bed and a taste for roses.

'Roly-Poly, get out of there,' Teesta hissed, convinced that the prince's grandmother would immediately order them both back home. But then a thorn pricked Roly-Poly, she squealed and backed away, and Teesta grabbed her harness.

'Come on, baby, up we go!' she sang taking a digestive biscuit out of her pocket and holding it in front of the rhino. She led the little rhino up the steps.

'Wow! Can I pet her?' Prince Shamsher asked as Roly-Poly peered around short-sightedly and snorted.

'Sure, she loves being tickled between the ears and on her chest,' Teesta said. 'But watch it—she's very strong, you know, she can knock you over like a feather.'

'Hey, will you take a picture of her with me?' the prince asked as they went into the huge Durbar Hall. He handed Teesta his camera.

'Sure, now go stand beside her,' Teesta said. 'By that window … you can put your arm around her neck if you like! Call her—here, give her this. She loves digestive biscuits.'

'Come here, good girl,' the prince called, holding out the biscuit. Roly-Poly sniffed the air and snorted. She saw the prince hold out his hand, from where the delicious biscuit smell was emerging. She tossed her head and cantered towards it.

'Roly-Poly, slow down. Shammy, dodge away. Her brakes are no good on this floor!'

Prince Shamsher dropped the biscuit and leapt nimbly to one side. Roly-Poly, now at full gallop, went past him and skidded wildly on the polished floor, crashing right into a gilded coffee table, upsetting the tiger rugs on the floor, which writhed as though they'd come alive. The magnificent silver vase on the table, filled with flowers, teetered and crashed to the floor and Roly-Poly hit the huge sofa and came to a halt. Still snorting, she turned and promptly snaffled up a bunch of carnations—ah, this was comfort food.

'Oh my God, are you all right?' Teesta called.

'I'm fine!' said the prince, quite shaken.

'Not you—I meant Roly-Poly!'

Teesta ran up to the little rhino and put her arms around her. She looked at the prince. 'I really think she'll be happier outside.'

'Yes, dear, I think you're right,' the prince's grandmother said, re-joining the children and eyeing the chaos. Palace functionaries were running around with brooms and mops, clearing up the mess.

'Let's take her for a walk in the jungle,' the prince suggested.

'We're not supposed to walk in the national park without an armed forest guard,' Teesta told him.

'I have my air rifle,' the prince said loftily.

'But you're not a forest guard or SRPG fellow.'

'That doesn't matter.' He looked at her. 'You know, in these holidays, I have to study rhinos and write a paper on them for school. It's my holiday homework. So I have to follow them about and observe them in their natural habitat.'

'Well, you saw them yesterday at the bheel.'

'Ya, we should go there again.'

'I'll tell Papa. He's on patrol today, but maybe tomorrow we can go there again.'

'I … I have to study them … alone like … With the elephants and guards around, there are too many distractions. The rhinos don't behave naturally.'

'Well, I think they were pretty natural yesterday.' She nodded. 'But I agree, it'll be more fun to watch them alone … No tamasha with the elephants and guards and all.'

'You were alone with Roly-Poly in the jungle for the whole night, weren't you? Dadiji said you wouldn't leave her … Were you scared?'

'Nah! How could I leave her?' Teesta lowered her voice and whispered in the prince's ear so Roly-Poly wouldn't hear and become upset. 'You see, her mamma had just been killed, so how could I leave her? I know what it feels to be an orphan …' She nodded knowingly.

'What do you mean?'

'My real mamma and papa were killed by wild elephants when I was a baby. That's when Mamma and Papa adopted me. So I know what it feels like …'

'Oh, I'm sorry …'

'But they're very kind,' Teesta added magnanimously. 'They give me whatever I want and hardly ever scold me.'

'You must know all the ways around the jungle here,' he said. They'd sat down on the sofa and Roly-Poly too had settled down for a snooze at their feet.

'Ya, pretty much! Papa takes me around quite a bit and so does Jawahar Singh.'

'So you must know where all the rhinos hang out? Like that big fellow we saw yesterday, who that other one chased away? Wow, how cool is that!'

Teesta blinked modestly. Whaddya know, the prince actually thought she was cool! Now how cool was *that*!

'Yeah, I guess I know where we can find him if we have to ...'

'Where?'

'Where he poops every day ...'

'Do you know where that big fellow poops?' The prince blinked and swallowed. Admittedly, it would be a bit silly to confront a rhino while it was pooping, to deliver it the coup de grâce, but it was at least a sure way of finding him. The little girl was looking at him curiously.

'Not right now, but I guess I could find out. Jawahar Singh knows these things. But why?'

'I'd like to see him poop!'

'Ew!'

'Yeah, disgusting.' He looked at Roly-Poly. 'You must have seen her poop.'

'Yes.'

'Where does she poop?'

'In the bathroom, where else! Where do you?'

'What? Eh?' For a second, he looked at her incredulously. Then he grinned. 'You're kidding me, right?'

'Well, we'd better take her out for a walk right now, or she may poop right here. Your dadiji won't like that.'

He grinned and she gave him a high five. He looked at her anew. She came up to his shoulders, had bright eyes and that bouncy ponytail. And she hadn't made fun of him at all. What a funny little girl. And brave too, if she had spent a whole night in the forest cradling a baby rhino.

'Come on, let's go ... I'll just call Mutthiji,' the prince said, as Roly-Poly gambolled around them. Mutthiji materialized and bowed.

'Ji huzoor?'

'Mutthiji, we're going for a walk in the jungle. Bring my air rifle and your gun too. And pack a hamper with food and soft drinks.'

'Ji huzoor.'

Teesta looked at the prince. 'Good, you're already dressed up like an Angrezi murgi-shikari,' she said innocently. 'Let's go!'

'Where should we go?' the prince asked as they left the regal palace, with its marble eagle-emblem gateposts. He slung his air rifle on his shoulder (it could really only scare sparrows and mynas) and placed the wide-brimmed Stetson at a rakish angle on his head. Mutthiji was properly armed with a powerful-looking rifle on his shoulder. He looked very strange, Teesta thought, what with his gold-rimmed round spectacles and chunky body, like a government office babu armed with a gun. Teesta clucked her tongue at Roly-Poly, who was trotting obediently at her side, hopefully anticipating another digestive biscuit.

'There's a pond nearby, another bheel, a little way off the road; we can go there and have a picnic,' she said. 'Roly-Poly can have a swim and wallow and cool off—she loves doing that.'

'What if we meet other rhinos?' the prince asked. 'It might be dangerous. You saw what happened yesterday.'

Mutthiji was talking into his walkie-talkie. Then he said, 'Roajer, over and out,' and switched off and looked at them.

'Theek hain—it's okay,' he said. 'I've just spoken to SRPG commando Hiro Da—he'll meet us at the branch-off, with his elephant in twenty minutes. It should be quite safe then.'

'Thanks, Mutthiji,' the prince said.

They walked along the dusty kachcha track for a bit, and were passed by several Gypsies and Jeeps carrying loads of tourists. Invariably these would stop; the tourists would gape and frantically take pictures, amazed by the sight of two children taking a baby rhino for a walk, accompanied as they were by an adult. Roly-Poly was nervous of the traffic and they would step well off the path when they heard the vehicles approach, but there was no really high grass here one could hide behind, so people saw them and stopped, their mouths falling open. Eventually Teesta got on her back and kept talking to her in that magic, gentle voice the little rhino found so soothing.

'Would you like to ride her too?' Teesta suddenly asked the prince.

He looked at her in surprise. 'What? Ride her? Won't we be too heavy for her to carry? And anyway, will she let me?'

'She's very strong,' Teesta said. 'And I don't think she'll mind! Come on, get up behind me.'

The prince looked nonplussed. If he didn't, she might think he was a wuss and he'd got enough of that from school. If he did, and the rhino knocked him off ... Well, at least no one could say he'd chickened out. Besides, it might be fun—imagine riding a rhino! How many of the louts back in school could boast of having done that?

'Okay,' he said, nodding. He handed his air rifle to Mutthiji and hauled himself up on to Roly-Poly's back. She squealed a bit, but then calmed down as Teesta spoke to her gently.

'It's okay, baby, I invited him. He's so skinny you must hardly have felt his weight. Come on, girl, giddy-up!'

Feeling quite proud (and wondering why), Prince Shamsher sat behind Teesta, tentatively holding her around the waist, thrilled to bits. The baby rhino trotted forward and he clutched on to her sides with his legs to keep his balance.

'Hold on to me, I don't mind,' Teesta told him, flashing him a smile. 'Soon you'll get used to how she moves.'

'Thanks,' he said.

'We'll get off this road in a few minutes and be in the jungle where these people can't come.' The tourists, alas, were not nearly as sensitive.

'By god, look at that! Two children riding a rhino like a bhaisa! Bachche, look this way, make the rhino look this way, one picture, one picture, one picture please. Smile! Pose, baby, pose!'

The prince stonily ignored them and Teesta simply made a face and comforted Roly-Poly, while Mutthi tried waving the tourists on.

They found Hiro Da on his elephant Rajkumari, waiting for them at the turnoff which led down to the waterhole about a couple of kilometres away. It really was too small a pond for full-sized rhinos, buffaloes and elephants (or crocodiles) to enjoy, but was just perfect for a little rhino like Roly-Poly. She gave a delighted squeal and charged into it, with the two children still perched on her back. Several gimlet-eyed pond herons and little egrets, who had been fishing, spread their wings with croaks of disgust and flew off.

'Roly-Poly, wait, let us get off!' Teesta squealed to no avail. The little rhino bounced into the water with a resounding splash, spraying muddy water all over the children.

After that, of course, there was nothing for it except to have a glorious mud bath. Roly-Poly rolled over and the children splashed each other, Teesta quite forgetting that she shouldn't be doing such things to a prince, and Prince Shamsher quite forgetting he was a prince as he splashed the little girl. On the bank, Mutthiji wrung his hands and squeaked in protest, but there was nothing he could do. Hiro Da just grinned and then Rajkumari stepped into the pond, sucked up some water and sprayed the children for good measure.

'Now you look like a proper murgi-shikari!' Teesta hooted. 'You've got mud all over your face and in your hair.'

'And you … you look like a chocolate gaindawalli!' the prince shot back, taking a fistful of gooey mud and dropping it down the back of Teesta's neck.

'Oooh, it's cold, but it feels so good!' she squealed, squirming with delight as the mud slithered down her back. 'Like melting chocolate ice-cream.'

'I've never had so much fun in my entire life,' the prince yelled happily. 'We must do this more often.'

'Any time you want,' Teesta said, her eyes shining eerily through her mud-covered face.

She glanced at him. She liked him. He was so unlike the stuffy, snooty prince she had expected. He was just a normal boy as gross as they all were who loved (like she did) a good mud bath and probably hated being a prince!

Mutthiji and Hiro Da sat together, smoking beedis, watching over them, while Rajkumari helped herself to wild grass, her tummy rumbling like a big diesel engine.

'Mutthiji, could we have the paranthas, please?' the prince asked, suddenly remembering the hamper and the fact that he was ravenous.

Mutthiji produced a nifty little gas stove, lit it, and started frying the paranthas right there. They helped themselves to the sizzling hot aloo and gobi paranthas and delicious mango pickle, eating hungrily. The prince eyed Teesta, munching away happily.

For a moment, he wondered whether he should tell her about his great plan. She knew a lot about the habits of rhinos, so could help him. But it was unlikely she would approve. She'd probably squeal on him and that would be that. He'd have to do this alone.

'What?' she said, sensing his look. 'Why are you staring at me like that?'

'Am not.' He looked away.

'Are too … Well, anyway, I wanted to tell you: Papa and I are going to take Roly-Poly into the jungle as much as possible this summer so she gets used to the place. We want to put her back into the wild where she belongs, when she can take care of herself. Would you like to come with us when we take her?'

The prince's eyes lit up.

He nodded. 'Thanks,' he said, his eyes shining. 'I'd love that.'

'I think we start tomorrow,' she said, taking another parantha—this one oozing with molten golden gur. 'Oh, yummy!'

Half-submerged in the pond, Roly-Poly flicked her ears and sniffed the air. What was that delectable aroma? Meetha paranthas? She loved them. She got to her feet, lumbered out and made for the children sitting on their picnic rug.

'Oh darn, she's smelt the paranthas!' Teesta squealed, scrambling to her feet. 'She loves them.'

'Are there any left?'

'One … yours really.'

'Well, give it to her …' the prince said, also getting up as the little rhino rolled determinedly towards them.

'You give it to her,' Teesta said, 'then she'll love you like she loves me.'

He held out the parantha—almost like it were a weapon—and the rhino snuffled it up, snorting happily.

Suddenly, Rajkumari trumpeted shrilly. Mutthiji and Hiro Da jumped up and scanned the area.

'Sher!' Hiro Da suddenly said. 'Bachche oopar—children, get up on Rajkumari.'

He was right. In the thickets at the far end of the pond, Baghbahadur, alpha-tiger of the park, lashed his tail in frustration. He'd been drawn to the area not by the scent of delectable children or even more delectable baby rhino, but by the sweet, oozing gur parantha. Ever since he had once dined on a goat that had just raided a mithai stall, he had developed a terrible sweet tooth. This morning, alas, he was not going to get his sugar high; the elephant knew where he was and was now rumbling, 'Get the hell out of here! On the count of three: one, two …'

Growling low down, he slunk away and continued his patrol. One day, he swore, he'd have his fill of sweet things—including that baby rhino.

Rajkumari relaxed and Hiro Da and Mutthiji decided that they should return to the palace immediately.

*

Tired, happy, muddy and very smelly, they got back to the palace early in the afternoon.

'Oh my God, what have you children been up to?' the prince's dadiji exclaimed as she watched them trudge up the driveway towards the steps, dropping globs of drying mud behind them.

'Roly-Poly wanted us to play with her in the pond, Dadiji,' the prince exclaimed.

'Stop right there! Don't take another step! Go into the garden and hose the little rhino down—and yourselves too. Then you can come in and have a proper shower. Oh my God, I can smell you all from here!'

They hosed the mud off themselves as best as they could, scrubbed Roly-Poly till she was shiny new and then went in to shower. The prince's dadiji handed Teesta a pair of the prince's shorts and a Superman T-shirt. In the broad verandah, Roly-Poly partook of a fruit and vegetable basket and then slept.

That night, after his dadiji had tucked him into bed, the prince had an unexpected visitor.

Mutthiji knocked deferentially on his door and entered.

'Huzoor,' he said, standing at the end of the prince's bed, adjusting his pink turban. 'If I have permission to talk? May I have a word with you?'

Shamsher looked at him warily. Was he about to get a lecture about how it was not proper that a prince should be frolicking in a muddy pond with a grubby little girl and baby rhino? He nodded.

'Sure,' he said

'Um … huzoor, there is talk … the subjects are talking … and are becoming restless …'

'Subjects? What subjects?'

'Your subjects … in the kingdom …'

'Kingdom? Mutthiji … you know …'

'Ji hanji, huzoor—yes, I know, there is no kingdom as such, but you know there actually is one and will always be one. The people still regard your gracious father as the maharaja and themselves as his loyal subjects. They know only he will look after them in their hour of need. But they are upset …'

'Upset? Why?'

'Huzoor, you know about that ancient ceremony that all maharajas in this region conducted when they ascended the throne?'

'Which one?'

'The tarpan …'

The prince nodded. 'Yes, Dadiji told me all about it. How Daduji killed the most ferocious rhino with a throwing knife …'

'Yes,' Mutthiji swallowed. 'But huzoor, the subjects are saying that your noble father has not yet conducted the great ceremony, which gives peace to his ancestors. He should do so, he should have done so by now but spends all his time in … clubs abroad …'

Prince Shammy's heart began beating fast. Just where was Mutthi going with all this?

'So? Papa knows … and anyway Dadiji forbade him to do it …'

'Yes, but it is not for her, a mere woman, to forbid him from conducting an ancient ritual as this.' He paused. 'But huzoor, a suggestion has been made …'

'What?' the prince barely dared to breathe. 'What suggestion, Mutthi?'

'It has been suggested that if you can conduct the ritual on behalf of your father …'

'Me?' the prince whispered. 'They want me to conduct the ritual? But …'

'Ji huzoor, I know, your esteemed father is still alive and may he live and drink and dance for more than a thousand years, but you will only be doing it on his behalf because he is … unable … to do it himself! And all backup needed will be provided …'

'They want me to kill a rhino and offer its blood for Daduji!'

'Ji huzoor. It's known that you are only twelve years old, but kings as young as fifteen have led armies into battle and you do not lack courage … Alexander the Great took charge at the tender age of sixteen and look what he achieved! And Napoleon was five foot zero!'

But this was just amazing—it fitted so perfectly with what he had been planning and had been desperately trying to plot. If Mutthi could provide the vital logistics for the hunt, all his problems would be solved.

Now Mutthiji nodded. 'It is against the Government's laws, maybe, not our laws, not the ancient laws that govern the kingdom of Gaindagunj! Besides, we shall ensure that no one knows. The Forest Department, the SRPG, shall know nothing of it. When the rhino dies, they will think it is just another kill by poachers! We shall take its horn too, to further that suspicion.'

'I shall need a proper gun,' the prince said. 'My air rifle won't be any good against a rhino.'

'It shall be provided, huzoor. I have custody of the keys of your noble father's gun cabinet.'

'But … but how exactly do we go about it?'

'Huzoorji, a rhino has already been selected. You know that rhino we saw at the bheel yesterday; the fellow who was doing handbrake turns to impress the ladies?'

'Yes. I think he's called Hulla.'

'He's the fellow.'

'And how? Where? When?'

Mutthiji noted the excitement, even tears glimmering, in the princes' eyes. The mahseer had been hooked!

'Do not worry about all those petty details, huzoorji. I shall plan it all. But suffice to say, no one must learn of the plan, lest they interfere.'

Prince Shammy nodded and gulped as if swallowing a lump in his throat.

'You know, Mutthiji, I had been planning to do something like that … to … to impress Papaji. And I had thought of the exact same rhino as the target. Papaji doesn't care two hoots about me and thinks I'm a pyjama. I couldn't figure out how to do it, but now, if you can plan it and set it up …' He sat up in bed and hugged Mutthiji. 'After I kill the rhino and crawl inside its belly and offer its blood to the gods for the peace of Daduji's soul, no one will make fun of me again. Dare they!'

Mutthiji patted the prince comfortingly on the shoulder.

'You know, Mutthiji, tomorrow I shall be going with that little girl Teesta and her baby rhino into the jungle with Commander Thapa. I've already told her that I have to observe and study rhinos for a school project. So I'll just do that and find out all I can about Hulla and what his habits are.'

'Ji, huzoorji, that would be very helpful indeed.'

There was just one cloud on the horizon. The prince was pretty sure that Teesta, let alone Commander Thapa, would not approve of his killing a rhino. And like it or not, she had become his friend and he liked her.

But all the same, he could not be treated like a pyjama any longer—by his father or the louts at school. He wrestled with his dilemma and eventually fell asleep as Mutthiji backed out of the darkened room.

4

'Papa, do you know where Hulla poops?' Teesta asked her father at the dinner table that night.

Her mother frowned.

'Rani, not at the table ... please!'

'Sorry, Mamma, but it's important!'

'And why is it so important?' her father enquired, his eyes twinkling.

'Oh, Shammy, I mean the prince, you know, was asking me ... He's very interested in rhinos and has to do a holiday homework project on them.' She looked at her parents and added proudly, 'And he's asked me to help him.'

'That's wonderful, darling,' her father said.

'And it was so good of his dadiji to let you borrow the rajkumar's clothes. The next time you go to play with him, I'll pack a spare set of clothes for you.'

'We had such fun!'

'We'll take Roly-Poly out again tomorrow to Akash bheel. She must get used to the jungle and its unpredictable ways as soon as possible,' said Commander Thapa.

'I hope that ruffian little boyfriend of hers is there too. She must play with other rhinos her age,' Teesta said seriously. 'She must learn to make friends with her own kind.'

'She will, don't worry … she's still a baby.'

'So can we check out Hulla tomorrow?' Teesta asked.

'We'll see. We can't take Roly-Poly along with us when we do that—it could be dangerous.'

'Maybe we could leave her with her boyfriend and pick her up when we return.'

'Better would be to leave her with Bakrasahib. He knows how to look after her. So, here's the plan: early in the morning we all go to the bheel, and return home for late breakfast. We leave Roly-Poly here and go back looking for old Hulla at around ten, ten-thirty.'

'That's great, Papa!'

What Teesta did not know was that Commander Thapa had had a tip-off that Hulla was the next target of the poacher's gang and he was keen to give the great rhino all the protection possible. Hulla's horn was magnificent and probably priceless. If anything happened to him, he, Commander Thapa would have to resign his post and hang his head in shame.

*

It was a quiet and peaceful evening at Akash bheel. A three-quarter moon dodged behind scudding clouds and the bullfrogs were singing drunkenly about love. Gaindaben and Rumble-Tumble grazed peacefully along the bank, watched over by a commando of the SRPG, mounted on an elephant. There were four other female rhinos in the vicinity of the bheel, also under armed guard.

'Stop sulking!' Gaindaben told Rumble-Tumble exasperatedly. 'I told you she was not for you. Make friends with that sweet little Srilata instead … that one is probably going to be deposited in some zoo once she's old enough. It'll serve her right for sucking up to human beings.'

Rumble-Tumble had been upset because Roly-Poly had not shown up the entire day (she had gone to the palace), and he had waited for her, getting more and more cantankerous as the hours went by. Of course, his mother would never know how he felt—and she couldn't see (she was short-sighted yes, but was she totally blind too?!) what a pretty little rhino Roly-Poly was, and how cutely her ears waggled and lips twitched and tail whisked. He'd been so stupid. He should have followed her that evening, when she left, escorted by those elephants. Just imagine, he didn't even know where she lived! He sighed and stomped his foot in the water, causing a night heron to flap away with an annoyed 'quaaark'.

'Watch where you put your feet, buster!'

'Sorry!' He backed away, too despondent even to mock charge it just for the heck of it. What if Roly-Poly never came to the bheel again? What if he never saw her again for the rest of his life? What if, as his mamma had said, she were taken to that ghastly place they called a zoo? No! He would never let that happen to her. He would free her and rescue her! She should run free by his side here in Gaindagunj. But first, of course, he would have to find her. He peered at the dim shapes of the night herons and black-winged stilts and painted storks feeding industriously in the water. Maybe they would know; they flew around everywhere and could see for miles around them.

'Er … sir, ma'am, excuse me … have you seen a little girl rhino, very pretty, anywhere nearby here in the park? She's usually escorted by elephants with human beings on their backs. A little girl is with her too …'

'Eh? Ha-ha! Your girlfriend dumped you, did she? What did you do to gross her out?'

'Um … no, ma'am, nothing! She doesn't even know that … she's my girlfriend … and I … I just want to prevent her from being imprisoned and tortured in a zoo for her whole life …'

'What?' the night heron eyed him, its ruby eyes boring into him. 'Is she going to be jailed for life?'

'Probably! And tortured too. They'll probably extract her horn with giant pliers.'

The birds murmured for a while between themselves.

'Um … ahem, she was seen at the Chhoti Talao this morning in the company of one elephant and four numbers of humans including two numbers of children. She was playing in the water with them.'

'Where did she go afterwards? Did you see?'

'Don't know, but she's been seen in the enclosure of the SRPG headquarters, playing with the little girl. The little girl actually rides her like a tattu pony! So degrading, really! I mean it's different when we ride on you guys—we take all your nasty ticks out for free!'

'How far is this place?'

'On your fat stubby legs, it should take you about half an hour—if you can trot for so long.'

'Thanks!'

Rumble-Tumble made up his mind. Tomorrow he would, for the first time ever, leave his mother's side and set off for the SRPG Headquarters and daringly rescue Roly-Poly. If ever there was a damsel in distress, it was her! He made his way back to his mother's side and nudged her.

'You want another milkshake? Baba, you're getting too big for this sort of thing.'

Ah, yes, he thought, but it may be the very last drink of milk he ever took from his mother. Tomorrow at first light, as she dozed ... he'd be off!

Alas, Rumble-Tumble grossly overslept. It was eight o'clock by the time his mother nudged him awake. It was a wonderful dappled sort of a day; the sun would emerge from behind big silvery clouds, shine down brilliantly and then just as it got hot, disappear behind the clouds. The breezes would cool you down like an open fridge door.

Oh, shoot—by now he and Roly-Poly should have been far away. He'd planned on taking her north, towards those big glittering mountains. There was a limpid blue water body he'd heard his mother talk about to Angel Wing, her personal little egret escort. It was called Hyacinth bheel, and was very secluded and near the river bank too, which seemed ideal. There they would frolic, and to hell with everyone else.

And then he heard Maharani's great tummy rumble.

There, on the track, were two elephants, Maharani and Hira, with his beautiful Roly-Poly trotting between them. She had come back! She had come to him!

But would she come *with* him?

He snorted and trotted off onto the track, his ears swivelling and blocking out his mother's squeal of irritation. Roly-Poly was standing in front of Maharani, her ears tweaking this way and that. Up on Maharani, Teesta, the prince and Commander Thapa watched, as Madhav Rao steadied the elephant.

'Just imagine,' Teesta whispered into the prince's ear, 'he was waiting for her!'

'And she was looking for him!'

'His mother doesn't approve,' Commander Thapa remarked. 'Keep an eye on her. She might charge.'

Rumble-Tumble cantered towards Roly-Poly, who stood stock still, waiting. He came right up to her and braked in a cloud of dust, and tried to do a stylish handbrake turn as he had seen Hulla do, but fell on his side and rolled over.

'Ooof!' he grunted.

'Are you trying to impress me?'

He staggered to his feet and eyed her.

'No, I have come to rescue you!'

'What? Are you serious? Come on, let's play tag. You're it!'

'Hssst … I'm telling you, you are in mortal danger!'

'Oh yeah? From what? You? My little girl is sitting up there, Maharani and Hira are right here … The only danger I see is for you. Your mom back there has smoke coming out of her ears and nostrils and I can hear her snort. Boy, are you in for it! She's gonna peel your hide or what!' Roly-Poly did a delicate pirouette. 'I don't think your mamma likes me,' she sniffed.

He shook his head in exasperation. 'I'm telling you! You are in mortal peril! Those … those … people are going to put you in a zoo and torture you for the rest of your life. You'll be kept locked up in a small pen and be fed raw cabbages night and day, and then they'll hold their noses when you fart. They'll teach you to do tricks to amuse them.'

'What? Did you munch some bad spinach last night? As you can see, they bring me for walks in the jungle. I have a lovely comfortable stable and my meals are prepared with the strictest hygiene. A vet examines me every week. He says I'm doing great, except he wants me to lose a little weight.'

'Can't you see? They're preparing you for the zoo! They want to make sure you're in the pink of health. They'll sell you and get a big price. Or …' he went on darkly, 'or … they'll hack off your horn and leave you to die! Like they did to your mom!'

Roly-Poly's nostrils flared and her eyes widened with shock. 'What?' she whispered. 'But I hardly have a horn. And … and …'

'Oh, it'll grow, don't worry about that. They're probably watching it every second. And when it's grown nice and big, they will just hack it off, chop, chop! Or yank it out with pliers.'

'They did that … to my mom? I don't remember … I only remember waking up on something very large, and then the little girl's voice pacifying me. She held my head in her lap all night and sang to me and comforted me. I don't remember anything else … Besides, they've been so sweet to me …'

'They're just trying to win your confidence. One day, they'll bring a crate into your enclosure and ask you to get in. And then, bang, bang, bang, hammer it shut, hoist it on a truck and it's bye-bye forever!'

'But … but why did they want … Mamma's horn? Or mine?'

Rumble-Tumble came up to her and whispered something in her ear. Her nostrils flared and she snorted.

'What? No? You mean … I don't believe you! You're kidding me!'

'I'm telling you. They believe that without our horns, they won't be able to umm … have proper honeymoons or kids.'

For the first time in her life, little Roly-Poly blushed, if you could imagine a baby rhino doing that. Or even an adult one.

'But … but they're swarming all over the place … there are so many of them … surely all of them didn't use our horns for their honeymoons.'

'Well, a lot of them did and want to, which is why there are so few of us left and why our horns cost so much. Besides, they think our various other body parts can cure a lot of their foul diseases.'

Up on Maharani, Teesta squealed delightedly. 'Look, he's whispering sweet nothings in her ear! They're so sweet.'

'So … so, will you run away with me?' Rumble-Tumble asked at last. 'I can protect you!'

'What? Run away with you?'

'Yes. So you won't be caught in their nefarious trap. I know of a beautiful place.'

'What about your mom? She's throwing a hissy fit back there already.'

'She'll be fine. As it is, she told me I shouldn't be drinking milk anymore, so what's her problem?'

He looked towards his mother. Gaindaben had come up on to the path and was stomping her feet, her nostrils flaring.

'Will you get back here at once, you disobedient little boy!' she yelled at him. 'Or do you want me to come and get you?'

Bravely, Roly-Poly turned to face the furious rhino-mom.

'Ma'am, it's okay … I just wanted to be friends with him, that's all.'

'You ... you will NEVER be friends with him. You are friends with humans! You are out of rhino society forever. Stay away from my baba—you are corrupting him. As for you, Rumble-Tumble, you're grounded, young man! No mud baths in the bheel for a week!'

Rumble-Tumble had heard only one thing: Roly-Poly had said she had wanted to be friends with him! Suddenly the world was a glorious place! His fat mom could rave and rant all she wanted. He scampered about, tripped over his fat legs, fell over, got up and danced in sheer joy.

'Have you gone nuts or something?' Roly-Poly giggled, keeping a sharp lookout for Gaindaben. Actually, Gaindaben had only kept her distance because she had seen the warning glitter in Maharani's and Hira's eyes. And taking on two elephant-moms, even though they were foster parents, was not an option. Frustrated and furious, she stomped and tossed her head around. Oh yes, was her ladla baba in for a hiding or what! He was a disgrace. Already all the other rhino-moms had hastily led their little ones away, making them avert their eyes from the shameful scene that was being played out.

'Is he kissing her?' Srilata asked her mother in her high-pitched squeal, trying to look at the two from under her mom's belly. 'Let me see! I want to see!'

'Beti, come along—you shouldn't be seeing such things.'

At last Rumble-Tumble sobered down. 'So, will you run away with me?' he asked, panting. 'You must!'

'I … I don't know. Let me think a bit,' Roly-Poly said. 'But thank you for caring. I appreciate it. You've got into a lot of hot water for me.'

'Nah … no problem,' he said, tossing his head. 'She'll just beat me up black and blue, that's all. Been there, done that.'

'You poor thing!' She nuzzled him affectionately and back on the path, Gaindaben nearly burst a major artery.

'Keep your hands off my darling baba!' she yelled and lost her temper completely. She charged. Simultaneously, Maharani and Hira trumpeted shrilly.

'Stop right there!'

Gaindaben skidded to a halt in a cloud of dust.

'Listen, Gaindaben,' Maharani said in a kinder tone. 'You don't have to worry. The humans want the little one—Roly-Poly is her name by the way—to become a wild rhino like you all are. That's why they're bringing her here so often—to meet and mix with you all. So maybe it's good she's making friends with your baba—maybe he can teach her the ways of the wild.'

'What?' Gaindaben snorted. 'Then … then why don't they just leave her here and go home? Let her be a wild rhino …'

'Gaindaben, you know they can't do that. She's such a tiny little thing and has no one to look after her here. And, you know, Baghbahadur has a taste for baby rhinos.'

Maharani and Hira rumbled to each other.

'Would you like to look after her, Gaindaben?' Maharani asked, her eyes twinkling. 'If you give her some TLC now, and offer to adopt her, maybe the humans will leave her here. She's a sweet little thing really.'

Gaindaben shuddered. 'I have one brat to look after and that's more than I can handle,' she sniffed coldly. 'I'm going into the bheel to soothe my nerves, now.' She tossed her head and snorted. 'Baba, come along now. Bath time!'

'Go and take your bath, baba,' Roly-Poly teased. 'Don't forget to wash behind your ears! Will you come to the paddock where I give the little girl giddy-up lessons?'

'What?'

'The little girl usually brings me out into the enclosure early in the morning, before her mamma wakes up, for a quick giddy-up. You can visit me there.'

Yes, Rumble-Tumble thought suddenly. He could visit her there, help her break out and then run away with her.

Up on Maharani's back, Teesta was thrilled. 'Papa, she's really made friends with that rascal. It's too cool!'

'Yes,' her father smiled, 'she's learning how to socialize with her own kind, which is a very good thing.

And, in spite of the fact that the fellow's mother doesn't approve of her!' And he thought to himself, *It's always the kids who are ready to make friends, not the adults who always think they know better.*

'Wow!' the prince exclaimed. 'She's really leading him in a song and dance, isn't she?'

*

'So, Mutthiji, what's our plan?' Prince Shammy asked his faithful aide-de-camp as he tucked into breakfast at the palace a little later. 'How do we go about killing Hulla?' After breakfast, they would be picked up again by Teesta and her papa on Maharani, and go looking for Hulla.

'Very simple, huzoor,' Mutthi replied. 'Once we know where he goes for potty, we stake out the place. When he comes there, you shoot him and we conduct the tarpan ... All your father's sins will be forgiven and his spirit will achieve peace. One astrologer has even said that he will stop smoking, drinking, gambling and dancing with young ladies if you do that. So it is very important.'

'But won't the SRPG be guarding Hulla?'

'Yes, but I will take care of them. Once they realize that the tarpan is being conducted, no one will interfere. After all, most of their fathers took part in rhino and tiger hunts in the past and they'll know why, and won't say anything. It's an ancient tradition and most of them don't like that it's been stopped.'

'Oh, I hope so, otherwise I could be in big trouble.'

'Nothing to worry about, huzoor ... you leave everything to me.'

'Thank you, Mutthiji, I don't know what I'd have done without you.'

Yes, Mutthiji thought. Once the rhino is killed by this bachcha, ostensibly for the tarpan, the maharaja will be so shamed in the eyes of his people that he will be forced to abdicate. The crown would go to the prince, and he being a minor would have to be guided by Mutthiji who would ensure that by the time the prince became an adult, the treasury of Gaindagunj Palace would be empty, and he, a very rich, powerful man. The prince's grandmother, the rajmata, and his mother, the floozy maharani, being mere women would have no say in what went on and would abide meekly by his decree. There was, of course, another, even more attractive and likely scenario: that the prince would be killed by Hulla—who was the most notoriously short-tempered beast in the park—in his attempt to shoot him, and the playboy maharaja would probably be banished from his own kingdom in disgrace. His dollybird maharani would go with him, kicking and shrieking, and the old rajmata would be too broken and probably die of grief. And he, Mutthiji, would take over the kingdom (imaginary though it was) and the treasury (which was not). If anyone inquired why he hadn't discouraged the young prince from conducting the tarpan, he could say he had, but the prince had insisted and had sworn him to secrecy and he was not one to break his word to his liege. People understood and respected that sort of nonsense. And, as a bonus, they would take the rhino's magnificent horn and report to the Government that it had been the work of poachers, even though everyone would know that the secret tarpan had been conducted. No one would complain or ask for an inquiry.

Suddenly, Mutthi's eyes gleamed: perhaps he could *ensure* that the prince did not survive the hunt …

5

They set off from the palace on Maharani and Hira a little after ten. Teesta left a very disgruntled Roly-Poly in the large enclosure with crusty old Bakrasahib and told her to be a good girl and that they'd probably go back to Akash bheel in the evening again. Roly-Poly chased Bakrasahib around for a bit and then sulked. She didn't like being left alone like this. She knew the little girl didn't have to go wherever she normally went all day, because on those days, they didn't go to Akash bheel in the morning as they had done today. On such days, she played with her all day, or took her to the palace, or into the jungle. She didn't ditch her like this. It was not fair!

'She doesn't love me anymore!' she sniffed to Bakrasahib, who had wondered close and picked up a mouthful of hay. 'She's ditched me for that new friend of hers.'

'Well, what do you expect? He's a human being, not a rhino,' Bakrasahib remarked sardonically.

'And you're a buddha billy goat, so look who's talking!'

Bakrasahib chewed his hay thoughtfully and wagged his beard, his eyes glinting humorously.

'By the way, the egrets were telling me, you have a friend in Akash bheel? A little rhino friend? A boy … and you have a gargantuan crush on him!'

'Who told you that?' Roly-Poly swivelled around, snorting.

'Oh, one of the egrets—Angel Wing she's called, I think. She frequently rides on the back of his mother when she visits the Akash spa—the venerable Gaindaben, no less! Says the old girl is absolutely furious … um … is this what they call a "relationship" these days?' He grinned and winked horribly. 'Are you going to elope with him?'

Roly-Poly grew suddenly thoughtful as she remembered Rumble-Tumble's conversation with her, and his dire warnings. Maybe she should get another animal's point of view on the subject.

'Um … Bakrasahib, he told me that the little girl and others here are going to dump me in a zoo. Could that be true?'

Bakrasahib snorted. 'With human beings, you just don't know! My good self and the late Bakrisahiba—god be with her chops—had been slated for a biryani dish to celebrate the birth of the prince, but at the last moment, the rajmata took mercy and saved us. We were just kids at the time.'

*

Mutthiji as usual had accompanied the prince and brought along the picnic hamper and soft drinks. Hulla had been spotted in a grassy, swampy area, very near the Hyacinth bheel, on the riverbank, which was about an hour's elephant ride away from Akash bheel. A rickety wooden bridge spanned the river, which was wider, lazier and shallower at this point. The gate here, at the far end, had for long been broken and never repaired, and access to villages across was more or less open. The SRPG ranger keeping track of Hulla had reported that it appeared that the rhino had been contemplating crossing over because the paddy fields on the other side looked lush and inviting.

'He's very clever, sir,' the ranger had reported. 'He's not sure the bridge can take his weight. He approaches it and then stops when he puts his foot on it and it creaks, and goes back, snorting. If the villagers bring their cattle over into the park, he'll guess it can support his weight and go across.'

Often the villagers did bring their cows and buffaloes into the park to graze, illegally, while Hulla and other rhinos went over to their side for the same purpose, also illegally. Talk about the grass being greener on the other side!

They ambled along the river as it curved northwards and then east again, to the area near the Hyacinth bheel and met up with the ranger keeping track of Hulla. 'He's in the high grass somewhere there, right at the edge of the bheel,' the man said. 'He's been amusing himself playing with the ducks in the water all morning … like a child in a bathtub!'

A large flock of ginger-brown lesser whistling teal had settled in a patch of blue water ringed by a glossy green and lilac carpet of water hyacinth. The bheel was a lovely inland pool, separated from the river by high banks. At one end of the pool, a narrow jungle path went past it towards the rickety wooden bridge. At the other end of the bridge, the splintered wooden gate gaped open, hanging on a single hinge.

'What do you mean?' Commander Thapa asked.

'Dekho sahib, wait and watch,' the ranger said with a grin. 'Keep your eye on that patch of elephant grass where it meets the pond.'

Just as they were getting restless, the elephant grass suddenly shuddered violently. From its midst, Hulla emerged at full gallop, snorting and tossing his huge head. He roared into the water like a battle tank, sending water fountaining high on either side. The teals took to the air with their musical calls and circled wide, whistling happily like schoolboys. Hulla slowed down and submerged himself till only his ears and nose (and horn, of course) broke the water's surface and one by one the teals circled and landed, a little distance away.

'My God, the fellow is like a runaway tank!' Prince Shammy exclaimed, going a little pale. How would he ever find the courage to face this monster and shoot him? Man, he shook the ground when he galloped!

'Have you found where he goes for potty?' the commander asked the ranger.

'No sir, not yet. But he has a fairly fixed routine. Later in the afternoon, he'll go towards the Akash bheel again in the hope that the lady rhinos will be there ... It's like his spa and club, sir, he goes for socializing and R&R.'

'He got butted out of his club the other day,' Teesta chirped up. 'That old Gaindaben really showed him.'

'How tall is he?' the prince asked, 'and how much does he weigh?'

'He must be six feet tall at the shoulder and weigh maybe two and a half tons, beta,' Commander Thapa said. 'That's the weight of a Toyota Land Cruiser.' The prince quickly scribbled this down in his field notebook.

'Okay, children, you stay here with Maharani, Mutthiji and Madhav Rao—I need to discuss something with the ranger sahib.'

The two elephants stood close together and Commander Thapa stepped from one animal to the other.

'That fellow's gone to sleep in the water,' Teesta commented, looking through her binoculars. 'Those silly ducks are floating closer to him. Good for them he's not a crocodile.'

Yes, the prince thought suddenly. He would do it. He could just see it all: standing there, gun at his shoulder, all 4 feet 8 inches and 80 lbs of him, facing this 50 kmph-pounding two and a half ton, six-foot-tall monster with its 3 foot horn. He'd wait till the beast was almost upon him and the ground rumbled under his pounding feet … and then … one shot between those little eyes and that would be it. And then, they would cut him open and he would crawl inside the beasts' warm innards and collect its ruby blood and offer it to his father's troubled, if wanton, spirit. It would be so marvellous if Teesta could actually witness—and maybe even film—his deed, then she would know how much courage it took. He'd have to think of a way of getting her to accompany him, without knowing why, of course, until it was too late. What was the point of doing something so insanely brave if there was no one to witness and admire the deed? If this went on to the Internet, it would certainly go viral and he'd like to see the faces of Harbans and company at school when they saw it. Hah! Call him a wimp and a wuss, would they! Also, he knew that Teesta's presence would give him additional courage, for with her around, it would be impossible for him to back out! If he was killed in the attempt, well, so be it ... only, it would be nice if he had time to whisper his last three words in her ear before dying.

'Hey, you're going all red again—has something bitten you?' Teesta eyed him curiously as he snapped out of his daydream.

'Uh ... no ... nothing ... sorry,' he mumbled.

'Sorry? What for? You are wacko!'

Commander Thapa came back on board Maharani. 'Okay, children, I have to go now ... you can stay here for a while with Mutthiji and Jawahar Singh on Hira and watch Hulla, or you can return home. The ranger, of course, will remain here to keep an eye on Hulla.'

'Okay, Papa. We'll stay for a bit.'

A little while later, the ranger suddenly pointed towards the bridge and said, 'Dekho—look!'

A herd of water buffaloes had started crossing the rickety wooden bridge from the village side, rattling the planks, with two small children, a girl and a boy, maybe ten or eleven years old, perched on the backs of two animals. Sill deep in the water, Hulla's ears flicked and his eyes broke the surface as he heard the clatter of hooves on the bridge.

'Those villagers have sent them across to graze; in the evening they'll go back,' the ranger explained. He spoke urgently into his walkie-talkie.

'What are you going to do?' Teesta asked him.

The man shrugged. 'I've informed the headquarters but there's not much we can do. If we try to round them up, they'll say the guards beat up the children—so there'll be trouble.'

There already was trouble brewing. Hulla had heaved himself out of the pond and watched the buffaloes as they came across the bridge on to the park side. Then, purposefully, he headed for the bridge. Before the guards and the elephants could do anything sensible to cut him off, Hulla had pounded over the bridge as it creaked and shook and bits splintered off it. Hira, giving chase, braked to a halt just before reaching it and raised her trunk and trumpeted in frustration. At the other end, Hulla turned around and stared snootily at the elephant, then trotted off down the path towards the village before suddenly veering off towards a wheat field.

'Oh God, there'll be chaos,' said Teesta, 'once he gets into the fields!'

The ranger came alongside on his elephant. 'Chal, we follow!' he said, beckoning to Jawahar Singh, and urged his mount into the river. 'We'll wade across—we have to stop him and bring him back.'

The mahout and Jawahar Singh nodded and they guided Hira into the water. Mutthi looked nervous. 'Is it safe? Just remember; huzoorji is with us!'

Hira was now more than tummy deep in the water, stepping carefully, and following the ranger's elephant.

'Wow! This is so cool,' Teesta said, thrilled.

'It's fine,' Jawahar Singh said. 'Hira knows she has passengers on her back and will turn back if it gets too deep.'

'Can elephants swim?' the prince asked, keeping an eye on the water level. They had reached the deepest section of the river and the water was just about lapping at their feet. It was quite scary, like being marooned on a moving island that was gradually going underwater at the same time! Hira moved on unperturbed, her trunk upraised like a snorkel. Ahead, the ranger's elephant had started pulling out of the water.

'Oh yes, they can swim. Can you?' Teesta asked wickedly.

'Sort of!'

'Don't worry, I know lifesaving tactics,' Teesta went on helpfully. 'Papa taught me. He says anyone who lives in places like this must know such things.'

'Whew, we've reached,' the prince said as Hira lumbered out of the water and trumpeted.

A group of villagers rushed agitatedly towards them, shouting.

'Gainda! Gainda! Rhino, rhino!' they yelled, gesticulating and pointing towards an adjacent field. 'Chane ka dal kha raha hain—he's eating all the chickpeas!'

'Oh god, can you imagine how much he'll fart now!' Teesta snorted.

Hulla indeed was feasting on one of his favourite foods. He could hear the villagers' cacophony behind him and cared two hoots about them. Deeper into the fields he went, munching away. Occasionally he would turn around and look at them and snort. He even mock-charged them once, as they fled in disarray.

Then a villager did a very stupid thing. He lit a firecracker and threw it at Hulla. It burst just behind him and that was it. With a bellow of rage and fright, the big rhino charged out of the field straight onto the main village path. Women and children screamed and fled indoors as Hulla paused, snorting wildly, ready to mow down anything in his path. A chicken squawked and foolishly fluttered across the road (no one knows why, perhaps to get to the other side). Hulla put his head down and charged, shaking the drying dung off the walls of the villagers' huts. He barrelled round a bend and then:

'Beta, khamosh ho jao—son, be calm! Sab theek ho jayega—everything will be all right!'

The voice was calm, serene and cool, as comforting as the waters of the Hyacinth bheel.

Hulla jolted to a halt in a cloud of dust and peered in front of him myopically. Right there, relaxing in the middle of the lane, was a large black and white cow. She gazed at him placidly, her knobby knees tucked under her, her dark sloe-eyes huge and lustrous. 'Puttar, you may call me Mataji,' she went on.

'Wha…? Who?'

'I am Sidhvi Gau Mataji from Kolkata. I spent ten years chewing the cud, meditating and doing yoga in the middle of Howrah Bridge … I must have calmed at least a hundred million people who were getting late catching their trains. What advice do you require, beta? What is troubling you? Would you like to learn and practice yoga to achieve eternal peace and bliss?'

'Yo … yo … yoga?' Halla snorted, completely at a loss. Normally cows and buffaloes got out of his way pronto. This one just gazed at him placidly out of those enormous eyes of hers. 'Nn… no, I'm fine,' he snorted.

'What is troubling you, beta?' she asked again.

'Aren't you scared of me?' Hulla snorted, recovering somewhat. 'Most cows just kick up their heels and run away, and are too traumatized to give milk for a week after meeting me!'

'Beta … I have dealt with manic truck and bus and taxi drivers on Howrah Bridge. Now, what's troubling you?'

'Gaindaben!' he suddenly blurted, and nearly bit his tongue off. 'She bothers me.'

'Ah yes,' Mataji said calmly, 'I know her. She consults me for anger management counselling once a week at the Akash bheel.'

'She does?' He snorted. 'Hasn't had much of an effect—she butted me just the other day. You can't be very good.'

'Beta, these things take time … Now take in a deep breath and hold it, and at the same time, stretch your left rear leg backwards and your right ear forwards as far as they will go. Now exhale very slowly through one-and-a-half nostrils … no, no, beta, try not to fart … hai, mai mar gayee—oh god, I'm dying! What have you been eating?'

'Wha…?'

Hulla tried it and nearly fell flat on his face. He heard a snicker behind him and swivelled around. Hira and the ranger's elephant had caught up with him and were watching him; the humans with open-mouthed astonishment, the elephants with amusement.

'Sorry. Another time, Mataji, have to go,' he muttered. He eyed the elephants, his ears twitching irritably.

'What are you looking at? Can't you leave me in peace? I was doing yoga! What's your problem? And anyway, there's enough here for all of us—help yourselves! Wheat, rice, dal, sugarcane, pulses, even arrack …'

'Move it, Hulla!' Hira rumbled. 'Get back over the bridge. You're trespassing!'

'The hell I am. In my father's time, all this land was ours. These greedy humans grabbed all the forest from us and cut them down and planted fields. So I have the right to feed here and wherever I want.' Hulla lost patience and rolled threateningly towards a group of village men who were brandishing sticks at him, yelling. They dropped their sticks and fled.

'Pah!' Hulla snorted.

'Chal, Hulla, hutt! Move, Hulla!' Jawahar Singh yelled from the top of Hira.

'Oh wow! This is so exciting!' the prince exclaimed, beaming at Teesta. 'We're actually herding a wild rhino back to safety.' For a moment he had forgotten what he had planned to do to that same wild rhino.

'You know, Papa caught Hulla and Gaindaben honeymooning once—I think that little hustler Rumble-Tumble might be his son,' Teesta said.

'Oh!'

Hulla rumbled over the bridge back into the park as the two elephants crossed the river again. Regardless of the tamasha, he had managed to consume a fairly hefty quantity of chane ki dal and cabbage, and its effects were soon beginning to be felt. He paused and looked at the little hyacinth pond with is flock of friendly ginger ducks. He liked this place. It was peaceful and secluded in spite of the fact that the village lay just beyond the bridge. In fact, that was a bonus because he could quietly steal into the fields at night and help himself to the variety of greens growing there. And there was that yogic cow that had somehow soothed his irascible mood, even if for a very short time. Perhaps he ought to go back some time and take up yoga and meditation seriously. Maybe then Gaindaben wouldn't biff his behind—though she was getting counselled for anger management too! But yes, he liked the place, and it was time he staked it as his own territory.

There was only one path that wound its way off from the jungle towards the Hyacinth bheel, and here, about twenty metres inside, at the apex of a bend and at the base of a large peepul tree (which would forever be grateful) Hulla raised his tail and marked his territory in no uncertain manner. Any other rhino wanting to wallow in Hyacinth bheel would have to use this path too and would know immediately that it was private property. Hyacinth bheel was out of bounds for them.

Up on Hira, Teesta and Prince Shammy were riveted to their respective binoculars.

'Look!' Teesta whispered excitedly. 'He's marking his territory. This is his spot now! He'll come here every day to do it.'

'Wow!' The prince felt a clutch of excitement grab his stomach. He exchanged a quick glance with Mutthiji, who nodded faintly. He too had realized the importance of what they had just seen. Now the plan could proceed swiftly. He scanned the path and its surrounding areas. The peepul tree was perfectly placed. The rhino would be directly below—no chance of a miss from here! He would put the prince on the broad branch above, armed with a heavy gun loaded with a blank. The noise and flash would make the rhino panic. And the recoil would be powerful enough to knock the skinny prince off his perch, down onto the track.

Directly into the path of the panicked rhino which would, of course, charge!

End of story.

Except that he would then step out from the cover and give the rhino the coup de grace with a heavy calibre bullet and let the villagers know that the royal prince had been killed in his valiant attempt to perform the sacred tarpan (which, he, Shri Mutthiji and loyal acolyte had had to complete). After that:

All hail Mutthiji!

6

'You're not to leave my side. You've been enough trouble this morning,' Gaindaben told Rumble-Tumble later that same morning, nudging him into the water while checking where Smiley Masi was, at the same time. 'My nerves are shattered. Thank God I have a session with Sidhvi Gau Mataji this afternoon.'

'Can I go for a walk by myself at least?' Rumble-Tumble asked. 'You keep saying I should be independent, but you don't let me go anywhere by myself.'

'You're too irresponsible. Next thing I know you'll be making friends with a piglet.'

'They're fun to chase,' Rumble-Tumble admitted. 'They run squealing, with their tails up.'

Rumble-Tumble wallowed in the cool water, thinking. Somehow he would have to get away from his mother. It didn't seem possible during the day. She was always hovering by his side like an enormous shadow. She wouldn't let him out of her sight. At night then, when she dozed off. Or even better, when she was distracted by Hulla next … He would slip away and make for Roly-Poly's enclosure as fast as he could. He tossed his head. Yes, maybe he'd even bash open the doors to her cell to rescue her, if it was necessary. And then the two of them would make for the Hyacinth bheel. He didn't quite know the way there, but that didn't bother him – there were so many animals and birds you could ask for directions. Now that he had an 'action plan' all thought out, he felt better. It was just a matter of taking his chance when it came his way.

*

'You must have got a lot of stuff for your holiday homework project this morning,' Teesta said to Prince Shammy as they perambulated their way back on Hira from Hyacinth bheel later that morning. 'I mean, we found out so much! We know where Hulla poops, we saw him raid the fields and play with those ducks …'

'Yes,' he said, 'and now I'll have to write all that up for my report.'

'Do you think Hulla will invite all the lady rhinos over to Hyacinth bheel now?' Teesta asked Jawahar Singh. 'For a poop party?' she added, dissolving into a reeling fit of giggles. And went on, almost in hysterics, 'And I wonder who the party pooper will be!'

The grizzled old commando smiled. 'He'll welcome all the ladies who come to the place, and go and visit those—like Gaindaben—who don't. But he won't allow any gentleman rhino there ... there will be a big fight if that happens.'

'Will he spend all his time there?' the prince asked.

'Knowing that badmash, he'll probably try and sneak back into the fields as soon as possible.'

Mutthiji too was pleased with the results of the morning. Now he just had to put his plan into action. It wouldn't be wise to rope in Hiro Da and his elephant Rajkumari, or any of the SRPG commandos, into the plot. Now that they knew where Hulla pooped and was likely to be, he could easily take a palace Gypsy and drive him there. Even if the prince had to follow the rhino on foot in order to shoot him, the recoil of the rifle would be powerful enough to knock him flat (if not out), and then the panicked rhino would do the rest. He now just had to decide when—it had to be soon, before the prince chickened out or changed his mind.

'We'll drop the rajkumar and you to the palace first,' Jawahar Singh told Mutthiji as they plodded back placidly. It had got quite hot, humid and prickly; rain seemed to be headed this way, but they were happy with what they had seen that morning.

'Roly-Poly must be really mad at me,' Teesta said, shaking her head. 'She must think I've ditched her totally.'

'Tell you what!' the prince suddenly said, looking at Teesta, his cheeks going a little pink. 'Why don't we pick her up? Then both of you can come to the palace and we can chill there again,' he suggested. 'It'll make up for leaving her alone for so long.'

'Thanks, I'll just ask Papa if it's okay.'

She spoke to Commander Thapa on Jawahar Singh's walkie-talkie and he said it was fine. 'Just be back home before it gets dark,' he told her.

Roly-Poly behaved like a proper little prima donna when they got home. It was only after being heavily bribed with a packet of chocolate-covered digestive biscuits that she 'agreed' to accompany (a giggling) Teesta and the prince to the palace.

'Such a good girl you are, such a sweet little thing,' Teesta crooned, using her special magic voice again. 'I'm so sorry we left you alone all morning, but we had to go and see that big bad old Hulla, and you know what he's like …'

Slobbering all over the biscuits, Roly-Poly snortily followed them, keeping close to Hira, whose eyes were glinting humorously.

Then they came to the path that led off to Chhoti Talao. Prince Shammy turned to Teesta and said rather wistfully:

'We had such fun there that day, mucking about … and I'm so hot and sweaty and itchy right now …'

Teesta looked at him askance. 'You want to …' she began. But it seemed that Roly-Poly had read their minds and suddenly remembered the fun time they had had there the last time. She veered off the main track and trotted off determinedly towards the pond, occasionally pausing to check if Hira was following her.

'Roly-Poly, not that way—we're going to the palace!'

Roly-Poly snorted derisively and cantered on—straight into Chhoti Talao, once again causing great distress to those venerable old fishermen, the egrets and herons.

'Oh God,' Teesta giggled wickedly. 'Now we have no choice, we'll have to get her out of there.' She grinned at the prince. 'And you know what that means!'

It was sheer bliss. The cool, soft, oozy, chocolaty mud on their itchy skin, great globs of which they stuffed down each other's backs and necks; and Roly-Poly splashing and ducking under, snorting away happily. At last, laughing and tired, they just lay back in it, revelling in its creamy coolness. On the bank, Jawahar Singh tried pacifying Mutthiji, telling him that kids naturally did these kind of things, and it was good for them.

Not terribly good really, because again, Hira suddenly rumbled. And there, parting their way through the high grass plodded a procession of palace elephants with fashionably dressed people on board, talking and laughing.

'Look, there's wildlife in the waterhole!' a shrill female voice squealed. 'Monkeys and ...'

'Baboons! No, they're chimpanzees ... and a ... what is that, darling?'

'Ooh, the smell—I think I'm going to faint!'

Poor Jawahar Singh and Mutthi leapt to their feet as if they'd been shot at, and bowed deeply.

Four gaily caparisoned elephants had arrived, carrying a royal safari party. The maharaja, in a sudden fit of whimsy, had decided to fly in some of his friends to Gaindagunj for a couple of days, and typically, neither he nor the maharani had thought it fit to inform anyone at the palace. They had arrived at the palace and set out on an 'elephant safari' almost immediately, albeit after a few drinks.

Mutthiji bowed deeply again. A tall bony lady with complexion like beige crepe paper, and wearing vivid lilac lipstick stared at him out of piercing close-set eyes which then swivelled to the two—or rather three—creatures in the water.

'Mutthiji ... what are you doing here and what are those ... creatures disporting themselves in the mud? Some new simian species perhaps?' She pointed towards the children who hadn't realized that they had company because of all the oozy mud in their ears. Besides, Teesta had just grabbed hold of a frog and stuffed it down Prince Shammy's shorts with a shout of glee. He rose with a yelp—jumped up and down, splashing mud all over her—just like you would if you had a frog in your shorts. Then suddenly both of them saw the gaily decked elephants standing on the bank, and the several posh-looking people gaping at them and taking pictures. At this moment the frog plopped out of the prince's shorts and Teesta had great difficulty in swallowing a mighty bubble of laughter.

'Oh God! Mamma and Papa!' the prince muttered, wiping the mud out of his eyes, so he could be sure.

'What?' Teesta asked, appalled. 'Are you sure?'

'I'm sure!' He suddenly grinned, his teeth glimmering white through his muddy face. 'But I don't think they know who we are as yet. If we duck under the mud, maybe we can escape!'

'Oh my God, do I have to bow or curtsy?' Teesta asked. The ooze under the prince's feet suddenly gave way and he lost his balance, his arms waving wildly. He grabbed at Teesta, clutching her for support, and they both fell flat in the water with a resounding muddy splash. Clutching at each other for dear life, they struggled first onto their knees and then their feet, trying to keep their balance.

'Water babies!' a woman's voice said in awe. 'Chocolate water babies!'

Roly-Poly was still making happy grunting noises as she rolled about and then scratched her back against a rock. The elephants in the royal party had knelt down, and Mutthiji, along with some palace functionaries, were now helping the guests to disembark. They were to have a picnic here and already other functionaries had begun setting up trestle tables and red-checked tablecloths, and opening the food and drink hampers.

The bony woman with the crepe-paper face and lilac lipstick was staring at the two children, still clinging to each other, swaying this way and that in the slippery mud.

'Who are those creatures, Mutthiji?' she asked in a voice like a pair of ice tongs closing together over your heart and squeezing it. 'They're stinking the place out—shoo them away!' She took out a tiny bottle from her purse and sprayed the contents over herself.

'Ranisahiba … they are Rajkumar Shamsher and his friend,' Mutthiji replied in a low voice. 'I tried to stop His Majesty but …'

'Shamsher? Nonsense! That's not Shamsher! He's scared of mud—never goes near the stuff!' the lady shrieked so that everyone in the royal party could hear.

'Shit!' Prince Shammy muttered, clutching Teesta's hand. 'My parents have brought their godawful friends over—all of Europe's leftover kings and queens, and hotdog and bubble-gum kings from America where they don't have any other kind. I'm royally screwed!'

'Will … will they banish you forever?' Teesta asked, 'for playing in the mud? If they do, you can always come and live with me.' She squeezed his hand and smiled. 'Mamma and Papa will be happy to adopt you too.' She gave him a quick, tight hug. 'There, don't worry,' she said, automatically using her magic gentle voice.

'Thank you,' the prince said, feeling a brief wave of warm happiness lift him up. 'But it's probably going to be worse than that!'

'Shamsher, is that you?' the woman called out shrilly, peering at him through her spectacles. She turned towards Mutthiji. 'And who's that … that thing he's holding hands with?' she inquired icily.

'Umm … jj… just some local village girl,' Mutthiji muttered, not daring to reveal Teesta's true identity for fear of what the commander might do to him if he did. Besides, it was true—Teesta was just a local village girl.

A large jowly man in a pink suit, purple tie and with bulging eyes came and stood beside her, his nostrils flaring.

'Eh? What? Where's Shamsher?' he asked thickly, emptying the contents of his glass and holding it up for a refill, looking around blearily. 'What are you talking about?'

'That … that … thing in the mud … Mutthi said he's Shamsher holding hands with a local village girl!' the lady said faintly. 'Maybe he's drunk!'

Other guests now lined the bank, staring at the children and baby rhino in the pond. Two tall slim blonde identical young girls began taking pictures with their iPhones. Meanwhile, the functionaries continued laying out the picnic as though nothing was amiss.

Then Roly-Poly decided to get to her feet, and sent an oozy wave rippling across the pond. She was right next to the children and they grabbed her for support. Roly-Poly ducked mischievously and rose, this time from right under the children. With them perched precariously on her back, facing each other and fighting for balance (and trying not to giggle), she waddled out of the pond, snorting.

'Shamsher! It is you! What is the meaning of this?' the bony lady shrieked, taking a step back in horror. Beside her the maharaja's face began going purple—the exact shade of his tie.

'Boy! You are riding on … what is that? A gainda? With a *girlie?* In the mud? You have shamed the Royal House of Gaindagunj!'

Roly-Poly really didn't like people who shouted. She put her head down, trotted briskly forwards and then butted the maharaja in his huge paunch.

'Ooof … aarrgh!' the maharaja wheezed, deflating like a punctured water balloon. 'Nuke it! Nuke it!' he yelped in a squeaky falsetto.

Roly-Poly veered away, and with the children still on her back, made for the trestle tables where sandwiches, canapés, salads and wine were artistically arrayed. She hit the salad bar first and then put her snout into a big silver bowl of punch, which contained pineapple juice fortified with vast quantities of vodka and gin.

'Oh no, she's going to get drunk! Baby, no, not that! You're a teetotaller, vegetarian, non-smoker and underage!' Teesta screamed, trying to steer the chunky little rhino away.

'Shoot it!' the maharani screeched. 'Shoot it!'

What? Someone else was now screaming at her, and at her beloved little girl! Roly-Poly wheeled around, bringing down the trestle tables and sending the guests scampering away.

'Do something!' the maharani screamed at her husband, shoving him in front of her as Roly-Poly cantered towards her determinedly. The maharaja, still wheezing and gasping, gave one look at the tubby little rhino with the two children still on her back, facing each other (and grinning cheekily) and shoved his wife hard. She reeled away backwards, straight into the muddy waterhole, followed by the maharaja. Roly-Poly stopped at the edge and stomped her foot, sending mud splashing all over the Royal House of Gaindagunj.

'What did she do?' Teesta asked the prince, watching the expression on his face. She'd been facing the wrong way, but he would have seen everything.

'She just splashed Mamma and Papa with muddy water,' the prince said gleefully. 'I love her!' So much so, that he leant forwards and pecked Teesta on both her muddy cheeks! Of course, he went completely scarlet after that, though, fortunately, there was too much mud on his face for anyone to notice.

Before things could get any worse, Jawahar Singh took matters in his hand. He urged Hira towards them and the elephant gently nudged Roly-Poly away from the pond.

'Come along, little one—you've had far too much to drink,' she said, rumbling affectionately. The children had slipped off the rhino's back, and stood clutching each other's hands, wondering what to do. Hira had an answer to that too: she picked them up one by one and gently deposited them on her back, and they lumbered away towards the main track and the palace. Behind them, Mutthiji and some of the palace's functionaries helped the maharaja and maharani out of the pond, while their guests reeled around, holding their noses (the mud did smell a bit), bleating and squealing hysterically. They had no idea that jungle safaris could be so dangerous or smelly!

The children arrived at the palace where Dadiji simply smiled at them and then herself turned the garden hose on them. She was getting quite used to this sort of thing and was happy to see the prince behave like a normal boy of his age. She knew she had been right to introduce him to that sprightly little girl and her baby rhino. The sprightly little girl returned home wearing yet another of the prince's Superman T-shirts and shorts.

Of course, there were repercussions. At dinner that night, Teesta took her place at the dining table as if nothing had happened, but stole glances at her parents, whose faces revealed nothing. Then the commander spoke up.

'I believe Roly-Poly wreaked havoc at the Chhoti Talao this morning, and ducked the maharaja and maharani.' He sighed and went on, 'Well, dear, the maharaja has ordered that she be sent to the Gaindagunj zoo as soon as it can be arranged.'

'What! No, Papa!'

'He's decided that she's become too familiar with human beings to be released into the wild. She attacked him and the maharani, so she might attack other people too when she's grown up.'

'Papa, releasing her in the wild would mean that she would never have to meet people ever again in the first place. And she's such a sweet-tempered little rhino. She won't harm anyone unless she feels threatened.'

'I know, dear, but what to do? They're saying it is for her own protection.'

'They can't do that. She'll hate it in a zoo! She's a free, wild animal—not a zoo exhibit. She'll die!'

'Well, she'll be well looked after and you can go and visit her as often as you like.'

'She'll miss her walks to the Akash bheel and … and her boyfriend … She'll be broken-hearted!'

'Well, dear, unless the maharaja changes his mind, there is nothing much we can do …'

'I can!' Teesta said, determinedly, angrily wiping the tears from her eyes. 'I know what to do!'

Soon after, she called Prince Shammy.

'Listen, your father and mother have sentenced Roly-Poly to life imprisonment in Gaindagunj zoo! You have to make him change his mind or I'll never speak to you again!' she blurted even before he could say 'hi'.

'Hi Teesta,' the prince whispered hollowly. 'Listen, I'm not allowed to talk or play with you anymore. They were pretty mad about what happened.'

Which was true enough. The maharani had expressly forbidden him to meet or play with 'that nasty, dirty little girl ever again', and the prince had assumed that she had known who Teesta was. The maharani didn't care a hoot about who the nasty dirty girl was, except that the prince was forbidden to see her ever again.

'Well, it was their fault for turning up like that without warning and making all that noise.'

'I know, but who's listening? And they think you'll give me all sorts of bad habits.'

Teesta giggled. 'I know. Papa said that everyone's saying we rode around naked on Roly-Poly!'

'What?' He sounded appalled.

'Just to spite them, next time we will!' she said hotly. 'But listen, you have to do something for Roly-Poly. You're the prince, after all … you must have some power!'

'I wish I did!'

And suddenly it struck him. He would soon have power. Once he saved his horrible father's soul, his father would agree to do anything he asked of him—he, Prince Shamsher, would have the power! And he would not send Roly-Poly to any zoo, perish the thought! She could live with Teesta as long as she liked and they could visit the palace as frequently as they wanted to, and have as many, even naked mud baths as they wished! He'd like to see his father's ugly face then! But first, of course, first, he'd have to kill that giant rhino Hulla and conduct the tarpan … Only then ...

And he had to do this quickly—before his parents and their awful friends went back to Europe or wherever. If he saved his father's soul in front of his friends, well, there would be no coming back from that, would there? And yes, he would take Teesta along with him when he went to do the deed—she would understand that it was the only way he would get the power to be able to set Roly-Poly free, so she wouldn't be so upset. Well, not too upset at least. That was a load off his chest—he really didn't want to upset her at all.

'Hey, are you still there?' Teesta asked, urgently. 'Or are you daydreaming as usual?'

'I'm there—I mean, here,' he said. 'Listen, I have thought of something … Can't tell you just now, but await my call. I have a plan.'

'Wow! I knew you'd help. I-L-Y-V-M!'

'What?' And when he figured out what that stood for, his face turned deep crimson.

'Umm … th… thanks so much,' he stuttered and disconnected.

Then he called Mutthiji to his room.

'We have to put this plan into action soon, Mutthiji,' he said. 'Before my parents and their friends return to Europe or wherever.'

'As you wish, huzoorji. We now know where the rhino can be found.'

'We shall be taking my friend Teesta along with us to witness the deed.'

'What? My lord, is that wise? You know how little girls might react in such a situation!'

But the prince was hardly listening. Another thunderbolt had hit him!

'Mutthiji,' he said slowly, 'do Mamma and Papa know that it was Teesta in the waterhole with me and Roly-Poly this morning?'

'I am not aware if they did, Your Highness.'

'Did you tell them?'

'No, Your Highness. I did not reveal her identity to them. I did not think the commander would have approved if I had tattled.'

'Dadiji didn't tell them either—she loves Teesta! So Mamma doesn't know … and they've forbidden me from playing with some nasty village girl who pushed me into the waterhole.'

'Huzoor, but they will guess very quickly who she was. Miss Teesta is famous around here for her rescue of the baby rhino and there are not too many little girls here who have baby rhinos as pets. They'll put two and two together …'

'Nah! When Mamma puts two and two together she gets twenty-two! Besides, we'll be careful to ensure that

Teesta and Roly-Poly are not spotted together by Mamma and Papa, so they won't make the connection. Anyway, it is my wish that Teesta accompanies me to the tarpan.'

'Very well, huzoorji!' Mutthiji thought furiously. The little girl could complicate matters; she'd probably get hysterical and he'd have to calm her down … but yes, she was quite a sharp little thing and she could work in his favour. She could vouch that the prince got knocked over by the rifle's recoil and was trampled to death by the fear-maddened rhino, which he, Mutthiji would then bravely dispatch, making him a hero. If the prince somehow survived, there would be two witnesses lauding his courage! He couldn't lose!

'Huzoorji, perhaps you should retire for the night now,' Mutthiji said respectfully. 'You know the maharaja and maharani will be taking their guests out on rhino safari to Akash bheel and other places tomorrow morning and you are to accompany them.'

The prince brightened. 'Will we be going with Commander Thapa on Maharani?'

'Yes, huzoorji.'

'Umm … thank you, Mutthiji.'

Prince Shammy waited till Mutthiji left, and then called Teesta.

'Listen, we're going on rhino safari to Akash bheel tomorrow morning with your papa on Maharani. Will you tag along with me?'

'Are you nuts? You just said that you're not supposed to see me or play with me.'

'Yes, but here's the thing: Mamma and Papa thought you were some village girl who made friends with me—they don't know who you really are. And they won't recognize you because yesterday you were all covered with mud! I mean, they didn't even recognize me. Dadiji never told them who you were—she likes you too much! And Mutthiji hasn't told them either. I think he's afraid of your papa.'

A slow smile lit up Teesta's face. It would be fun, she supposed. And yes, maybe if … then perhaps the prince wouldn't even have to put his plan into action. She would have to tackle her father tactfully.

'Papa,' she said sweetly when he and her mom came to say goodnight. 'Papa, can I please come along with you tomorrow for the safari? It'll be so exciting with all those hoity-toity people and all.'

'What? They're not your kind of people, sweetie. You'll get bored.'

'Prince Shammy will be coming along too,' she said. 'He asked me to come.'

'He did? The maharani allowed it? After what happened yesterday I'd thought they'd banish us all from Gaindagunj forever!'

Teesta's eyes sparkled mischievously. 'Papa, they don't know it was me in the waterhole with the prince and Roly-Poly yesterday. They think it was some simple bad village girl who was playing with him.'

'Oh …'

'I'll be good,' she said, 'I'll just sit quietly with you.'

'Bitiya, what will you wear? Every time you go into the jungle, you return with clothes that are covered with mud, or wearing the rajkumar's clothes.' Her mother opened Teesta's cupboard and vexedly began checking her clothes.

'Okay,' her papa said, smiling. He really found it very difficult to refuse her anything. 'We're going on Maharani as usual, and with Hira and Jawahar Singh. The other elephants will be from the palace and the tourism department—I refused to let them have any more elephants from the SRPG.'

'Yay, Papa! I love you! Goodnight!'

'I'm sure you do, baby, now that you've got your way, as usual!'

7

The chief guests in the maharaja's entourage were Lord and Lady Creamy-Bottom Blunderbuss of Creamybottomshire in England. Lord Blunderbuss was a florid fleshy man with a bulbous red nose whose grandfather had bopped off any number of tigers and rhinos in his time in India. Lady Blunderbuss, whose expression was like that of a dyspeptic camel, could, it was rumoured, bring a pack of slavering pit bulls under control with a single word: 'Sit!'

They, along with the maharaja and maharani, accompanied Commander Thapa on Maharani, the elephant, for the rhino safari the next morning. Prince Shamsher along with the Blunderbusses' freckled twelve-year-old twin daughters, Rosy and Posy (can you believe it!), and Teesta, looking very fetching in a blue and gold salwar kameez ('I look like a macaw, Mamma!'), followed on Hira with Jawahar Singh. Mutthiji was with other guests on the palace elephants. For several moments, the prince had just stared at Teesta open-mouthed after she had been lifted aboard Hira—he couldn't get over how pretty she looked.

Rosy and Posy were thin, blonde and blue-eyed. They wore huge straw hats on their heads and fluttered hand fans in front of their faces.

'Oh my God, it's so hot,' Rosy complained, fanning herself.

'That's why the rhinos love a mud bath,' Teesta explained, and then bit her lip. The prince grinned at her.

'He had a nice mud bath all right yesterday,' Posy said, looking at the prince. Then she stared hard at Teesta. 'Hey, weren't you the little girl he was playing with in the mud?' she asked. 'You were riding the rhino with him, weren't you?' she went on, grinning. 'Here, we have it on the iPod!'

'No ... no, that's not me!' said Teesta, shaking her head wildly.

Posy was having none of it. 'It is too! And you said you're Teesta and the princes' Daddyji (she meant Dadiji) told us that that was the name of the little girl who had rescued a baby rhino—and you were both on that baby rhino's back yesterday, so it has to be you!'

She sighed wistfully. 'You know, we have ponies back in England but we've never ridden a rhino.'

'It's easy,' Teesta blurted again and bit her tongue.

'I'd love to have a mud bath,' Rosy sighed. 'Mummy and Daddy would kill us, of course.'

'It's really cool,' Teesta said, 'and slushy.'

'Can you ... umm ... arrange one for us?' Posy whispered to Prince Shamsher, exchanging glances with her twin.

The prince nodded.

'I'll see what I can do,' he murmured, wondering how the heck they were going to pull this one off. 'You'll have to be prepared for trouble afterwards,' he warned.

'No problem,' the girls said, smiling prettily at him. 'Thanks so much!'

Much to Teesta's horror, Commander Thapa had proudly introduced her to the maharaja and maharani before they had set out. He really was the proudest father in all of India, he believed.

'This is my little girl, Teesta,' he said, 'who, as you may have heard, spent an entire night in a trap with a baby rhino in her lap! She saved its life.'

'What on earth for?' the maharani asked, genuinely puzzled. 'This place seems over-run by little girls and rhino babies, doesn't it?' she tinkled. 'We found Shamsher and that nasty little village girl disporting themselves in that waterhole with one just yesterday. Imagine that!'

Teesta's eyes grew large. 'Really? Oh, so it's true then!' She lowered her voice and continued, 'Is it also true that they were naked? I heard something like that. I hope His Highness didn't pick up any ticks or fleas from her!'

'Oh my God! Shamsher, you will have to be thoroughly fumigated and deloused when we get back.'

Teesta grinned mischievously at the prince who glowered back at her, but then her smile died quickly. The maharani was peering closely at her.

'She was such a nasty ugly little girl,' she said, 'covered with mud. Not pretty like you! I hope you'll be friends with Shamsher.'

*

Roly-Poly, of course, had been none too pleased at being left behind again with Bakrasahib. She was also being plagued by the darkest suspicions.

'They leave me alone every day,' she wept angrily. 'I'm sure she is going to send me to a zoo after all. Rumble-Tumble was right! He warned me. I miss him.' She looked around. Up ahead, a couple of blazing white egrets patrolled the enclosure, their eyes peeled on the ground for the slightest move of a frog or insect.

'Birdies?' Roly-Poly called tentatively. 'Birdies?'

'You talking to us?' One of the egrets ruffled his aigrettes and stared at her, his eyes boring right through her tough little rhino head.

'Yes ma'am … er … sir … how should I address you?'

'Sir,' the egret said coldly.

'Can you do me a favour, please? Can you fly off to the Akash bheel and let Rumble-Tumble know that I have to be rescued? It's an SOS situation!'

'What's in it for me?'

'You can pick all the plump succulent ticks you want off me,' Roly-Poly said primly. 'I won't flick an ear! And you can ride on my back or hop in front of me and snap up all the high protein, fresh, juicy, full-of-natural-goodness vitamins and minerals enriched insects that I disturb as I walk.'

'Very well, it's a deal. Message to be couriered to Master Rumble-Tumble, son of Gaindabenji, resident of Akash bheel, Gaindagunj National Park?'

'That is correct!'

*

There had been developments at the Akash bheel too. Early that morning, Gaindaben had awoken and nudged Rumble-Tumble awake. A soft long lowing hummed all around the bheel, like the inside of some gigantic bell.

'Mooooooooooommoooooooomm!'

'What?' She blinked blearily as Rumble-Tumble snorted and started on his first bottle of the day.

Hazy in the morning mist, Bhaisaraja and his harem stood on the banks of the bheel facing Sidhvi

Gau Mataji. Gaindaben looked at the wild buffaloes and shook her head exasperatedly.

'What's bothering you? You need milking desperately or you're going to burst or what? Sure, sounds like it!'

'Gaindabenji, be calm, shanti! We're chanting and meditating. Our blood pressure has been too high lately, and we requested Gau Mataji to give us becalming lessons …' said Bhaisaraja.

'Puttari, how is your anger management these days?' Gau Mataji inclined her head. 'Perhaps you could join us here—chanting will soothe your temper and set the mood for the rest of the day … And we can do some yoga afterwards.'

'Baba, why don't you amuse yourself for a while?' Gaindaben told Rumble-Tumble. 'I have my yoga class now. Just keep an eye on where Smiley Masi is, if you want to get into the water.'

'Oh okay … I know when I'm not wanted,' Rumble-Tumble grumbled, looking around. Alas, there had been no sign of Roly-Poly all of yesterday and even this morning. Suddenly, an egret landed on his back and he started forwards.

'Whoa! Easy boy!' the egret snapped. 'Are you Master Rumble-Tumble, son of Gaindabenji, resident of Akash bheel, Gaindagunj National Park?'

'Maybe. What's it to you?'

'I have a courier message from Miss Roly-Poly, resident of SRPG HQ, Gaindagunj.'

'You do? Well, don't just stand there picking ticks off my back. Tell me!'

'She wants to be rescued. By you! Now!'

'What?' Rumble-Tumble looked around. His mother had drifted towards the wild buffalo yoga group and was now trying to stretch her left front leg and rear right leg out at the same time without falling on her face.

This was his chance! Roly-Poly was in trouble and had asked for his help!

'Okay, but which way to SRPG HQ?' he urgently asked the egret.

'What do you think I am—your homing pigeon?'

'Please …'

'Hmph … the things I have to do for a few ticks and leeches. Very well, follow me.' The egret took off, gained height, circled around and headed west. Gamely, Rumble-Tumble followed, trying to keep one eye on it and another where he was putting his feet. Fortunately, he stumbled onto the well-trodden path which the elephants used and was soon trotting along determinedly, nodding his stumpy little head and chanting, 'I will save her! I will save her! I will save her!' as he went along.

He was a huffed-puffed-out little rhino by the time he reached the enclosure, where Roly-Poly stood forlornly, a wisp of hay hanging from the corner of her mouth. Poor Bakrasahib had had a hard time trying to pacify her, but he was a worried old goat too. He had heard rumours that Roly-Poly was to be moved to a zoo: he'd overheard some jungle mynas excitedly gossip about it. Apparently, they had been present at an incident at the Chhoti Talao and had heard the maharaja declare that the little rhino would be moved to a zoo because she was dangerous company. They had loved cleaning out Roly-Poly's ears and would miss her, but Bakrasahib had driven them away from the enclosure before they could tell her that they would visit her in the zoo at least once a week, so not to worry! He knew he would miss her too.

At the SRPG HQ, Roly-Poly had begun to fret when suddenly there he was, at the gates of the enclosure, his mouth and nostrils flecked with foam—her very own Rumble-Tumble!

'Roly-Poly!' he panted hoarsely. 'I have come for you!'

'About time too,' she said tartly but rushed up to him and nuzzled him gently. 'Hey, catch your breath, cutie-pie! You ran all the way?'

'Uh-huh!' he blinked. 'Did you just call me cutie-pie?'

'We have to get out of here. They're going to put me in a zoo. The little girl has dumped me. I'm so unhappy!'

'It's okay, I'm here! I have a plan. We'll go to Hyacinth bheel and chill there.'

'Hey, hey, wait a minute, sweetheart. Do you think it's all right to just go running off with that little ruffian?' Bakrasahib demanded, trotting up. 'I should think not!'

'I'm going,' Roly-Poly said stubbornly. 'Don't try to stop me, Bakrasahib.'

'And what will I tell the little girl when she finds out?' Bakrasahib bleated. The two little rhinos ignored him—they were staring at each other across the fence, nuzzling their stumpy little horns, making grunting-love noises.

'Oh my God, this is young love. True love! Like the love Bakrisahiba and I once had,' the old billy goat muttered. 'How can I now object?' He nodded. 'Go, my children—you have my blessings!'

'Incoming!' Rumble-Tumble yelled, backing off and lowering his head. He charged at the gate of the enclosure and blasted right through it, splintering the wood.

'Yay!' Roly-Poly cheered.

'Let's go, chicklet,' Rumble-Tumble said, trotting around triumphantly, his tail up. 'Hyacinth bheel, here we come!'

They trotted out onto the elephant track and then Rumble-Tumble stopped.

'Lead on,' Roly-Poly said. 'Why have you stopped?'

'Hey, you up there, Mr Egret Courierji, which way to Hyacinth bheel?'

The yoga cum meditation class had just got over when the Royal Rhino Safari Party reached Akash bheel. Gau Mataji had gone around blessing all her acolytes and then drifted away on her way back towards her village. Then, as Maharani stepped out through the tall grass, with the royal party on her back, all hell broke loose.

Gaindaben had discovered that Rumble-Tumble was missing!

At first she thought he was playing hide-and-seek with her. She looked around blearily, calling to him, and then got angry.

'Enough is enough. Now come out and eat your breakfast!'

Still there was no sign of him. She was just beginning to panic when Maharani appeared in her usual stately fashion.

Ah, those riding elephants again! They had escorted that no-good little girl-rhino who her silly baba had gone running after. Maybe they had somehow spirited him away. Gaindaben's temper shorted. She coldly eyed both Maharani and Hira, and pawed the ground.

'My baba! What have you done with him?' she snorted and charged.

'Eeek! The rhino's charging!' Ranisahiba screamed. Lord Blunderbuss raised an imaginary gun to his shoulder and went, 'Bam! Bam! You're dead!' He'd already had far too many gin-and-tonics.

'What the …?' the maharaja stuttered.

On Hira, the children stared in alarm as Gaindaben rolled towards them at full throttle.

'What's the matter with her?' Teesta said, instinctively catching hold of the prince and a retaining rope on the elephant. 'She's not stopping!'

'Can it capsize an elephant?' Rosy and Posy asked together, their faces going pale.

Both Maharani and Hira raised their trunks and trumpeted shrilly as Commander Thapa raised his real gun to his shoulder and prepared to fire a shot over the charging rhino's head.

'Ruko!' the mahouts yelled in unison, waving their arms.

'Stop right there! Have you lost your marbles?' the elephants trumpeted.

'Sittt!' Lady Creamy-bottom ordered, not in the least fazed. Poor Maharani and Hira nearly sat down straightaway on their big bottoms, but luckily realized in time that the order was not directed at them. Otherwise, there would have been chaos.

Gaindaben skidded to a dusty halt a few feet away from Maharani.

'Duh!' she said. 'Not lost my marbles, but my baba! Have you seen him? Are you hiding him? Have you kidnapped him? If you have …'

She stomped her great feet in frustration and prepared to charge again.

'She's very distressed,' Commander Thapa observed. 'Something's upset her!'

'These animals attack unprovoked,' the maharani moaned, fanning herself and spraying perfume all over her face. 'They're like Delhi's drivers! Let's go back to Monte Carlo.'

'Papa, that little ruffian rhino is not around,' Teesta suddenly called out to him. 'He's normally with his mom …' She had been looking out for Rumble-Tumble and naturally couldn't see him anywhere. 'Maybe a tiger got him, and that is why his mom is so upset.' Her face suddenly paled. 'Oh my God, what do I tell poor Roly-Poly when we get back? She loved him! This is such a tragedy!'

'We'd better move away from here now,' the commander decided. 'The natives are restive. We'll check out some other water bodies.'

*

At the Hyacinth bheel, old Hulla was master of all he surveyed. He'd had a rollicking time. A herd of sambhar and chital had come down to the bheel for a drink and a soak, and Hulla had come thundering out of the elephant grass and sent them scattering in panic. How he had roared with laughter, and above, his good friends the teals had whistled their appreciation as they circled around him, dipping their wings in salute. The foraging was excellent and, of course, gourmet fields lay on the other side of the river, at his disposal. His territorial dung heap had grown in heaps and bounds, causing great joy to a poor hard-working couple of dung beetles inhabiting the area.

If there was one problem with Hyacinth bheel, Hulla thought, it was that it was a little too peaceful. A self-respecting rhino needed to lose its temper and charge at least once every fifteen minutes or so; it kept the adrenalin flowing and the muscles well-toned. Here there was very little that could light one's fuse. It was, of course, the ideal sort of place for a highly-strung rhino like Gaindaben—who lost her cool (with him) once every fifteen seconds—so maybe she needed to come here and savour the place's tranquil ambience.

Well, he could always trot across the bridge and indulge himself in the fields next door while the villagers went berserk; that would liven things up. Besides, there was that yogic mataji cow too who intrigued him. He had heard that she held yoga classes at the Akash bheel for the water buffaloes and that Gaindaben consulted her too. Hah! Maybe he could go and see her and ask her to put in a good word for him to Gaindaben.

'Boy!' he ordered his paddy-bird assistant. 'Fly over the village and let me know if that yoga mataji cow is there. Tell her I need to see her. Better if she comes here. Make an appointment for ASAP.'

'Very well, sir.'

Sometime later, Hulla had been foraging peacefully when his ears twitched. The SRPG ranger's elephant lifted her trunk and felt the air.

'Visitors!' she rumbled sonorously. 'We have visitors.'

Up on Hira, the four children had become firm friends. Rosy and Posy had been completely blown away by Teesta's rescue of Roly-Poly.

'Can we make friends with her? Please?' they begged. 'She sounds like such a sweetie!'

'She is. But she's also pretty stubborn and wilful,' Teesta grinned. 'And she loves chocolate-coated digestive biscuits.'

'Ah, we're nearly there,' the prince said, hardly believing that he was reclining on the back of an elephant with three pretty girls. 'This is where old Hulla puts up. He's the big boss rhino of the park. The meanest, angriest, nastiest rhino here.'

'But that Gaindaben really put him in his proper place,' Teesta said. 'You should have seen him run!'

'What! More rhinos? We've seen enough rhinos for a lifetime,' the maharani complained to the commander. 'Can't you show us anything else? Penguins and koalas, bears wearing tutus riding bicycles perhaps?' The commander inclined his head.

'Ranisahiba, this is Gaindagunj National Park, remember … where we protect wild rhinos,' he murmured. 'Not Singapore zoo.'

'Really, if I had my way, I'd have the rhinos and other rubbish animals cleared out and introduced water sports, casinos and yachts here. Jet-boating, roulette and whatnot!' the maharaja told his guests. 'Really, this country has reached such a state that even a maharaja can't gamble in his own kingdom!'

'Bang bang!' Lord Blunderbuss agreed. 'That's the spirit!'

The children, on Hira nearby, overheard everything. Prince Shamsher, Rosy and Posy went pink with embarrassment. Only Teesta felt proud of her father. He was the protector of the rhinos of Gaindagunj.

'Look,' she said, pointing. 'There he is. Old Hulla—that's short for Hullabaloo!'

'Wow, he is huge! Why do you call him that?' Rosy asked.

'Because …' Teesta began, and then old Hulla promptly gave them a demo. He did a stylish reverse 'J' turn and pounded into the bheel, showering muddy water everywhere and sending the teals up into the sky, whistling cheerfully.

'He's just showing off,' Teesta grinned. 'He does that every time we come here.'

*

Back at the SRPG HQ, there had been rapid developments. Squinting and muttering under his breath, Baghbahadur, now on a quest for baby rhino, had slunk up to the enclosure where Roly-Poly had been penned with Bakrasahib for a quick dekko. The coast had seemed clear: all the elephants and staff seemed to be out on patrol. The place was deserted. But the door to the enclosure was open, broken open, and there was no sign of the little rhino. At the far end, the old billy goat regarded him nervously.

'Oye buddhe, where's the baby gainda?' Baghbahadur called.

Bakrasahib rolled his eyes. 'You can make seekh or shami kababs out of me! You can make malai kofta out of me! You can make Hyderabadi biryani out of me! But I will never tell!'

'Pah! Some malai kofta you'll make. Who wants to eat you—tough and stringy and full of gristle that will get stuck between my teeth, and then I'll have to floss and whatnot! Now, where is she?'

'She's gone. Never to return! With the love of her life!'

'What?' For a moment Baghbahadur debated whether to attack the buddha billy goat and then decided it would be infra dig.

'Where has she gone?' he growled.

'Don't know.' Bakrasahib had managed to balance himself on the fence railings at the far side. Now he had the advantage of height! If the tiger attacked, he'd be able to butt him off just as he had seen those bharal do on the National Geographic Channel.

'I'll find her if it's the last thing I do!' Baghbahadur put his nose to the ground and ear to the breeze. Sure enough, he caught the scent of the two little runaway rhinos near the gate.

'Two for the price of one!' he gloated, moving off, his nose twitching. 'This is my lucky day.' A little later, he had to move off the path when he heard the Royal Safari Party on its way back. Only the tip of his tail was spotted by sharp-eyed Teesta as he disappeared into the grass.

'Look! Tiger!'

All the elephants stopped, binoculars were jammed to people's eyes and Lord Blunderbuss raised his imaginary gun again and barked, 'Bang! Bang! Got the fellow!'

'Wow, he was enormous!'

'With slavering jaws!'

'Thank God, we've seen something other than charging rhinos.'

Teesta's eyes grew dark with anxiety as they reached the SRPG enclosure after dropping their royal entourage back at the Palace. The gate was open, Bakrasahib was meditatively chewing hay at the far end, but of Roly-Poly there was no sign.

It was Jawahar Singh who noticed the prints on the dusty ground near the splintered gate. Several rather confusing prints of baby rhino. And also, the clear pugmarks Baghbahadur had left behind on top of them.

'Teesta baby, she seems to have run away,' he said heavily. 'And that tiger is after her. He might have come here and made her panic …' He looked up at the stricken little girl. 'He hasn't killed her—see he's following her …'

'We saw a tiger on the way back!' Teesta cried. 'It must have been him. We've got to follow him and save her. She must be so scared, poor little thing. I should never have left her alone!'

Just then there was a startlingly loud crack and blinding flash of light, followed by a great rumble of thunder. A silver curtain of rain descended as they rushed indoors.

'Oh no,' Teesta wept. 'The rain will wash away all tracks. We'll never find her again!'

Jawahar Singh patted her head. 'Teesta baby, she is a rhinoceros and she gets top protection here. I'll organize a proper search with your papa once the rain stops. We'll find her.'

Find her, they would.

Dead or alive?

That was the question.

8

'Are you sure you know the way?' Roly-Poly panted as Rumble-Tumble charged through the high grass vaguely in the direction the egret had indicated.

'Ya, he said turn this way, that way and then go, go, go!' Rumble-Tumble yelled back.

'Are you sure? I thought he said turn that way, this way and go, go, go!' Roly-Poly yelled back.

'Hey, look, there's another waterhole there. Last one in is a dodo!'

The two baby rhinos veered off the path and charged into the small waterhole Rumble-Tumble had spied. They couldn't resist a waterhole when they saw one. They splashed in and rolled blissfully in the mud.

'Wow! We're free!'

'This is such fun!'

At last, tired, they lay side by side, cooling off.

'My mom would bust a gut if she knew where I was and what I was doing,' Rumble-Tumble snorted.

'And who you are with,' Roly-Poly added tartly. 'She didn't like me one bit.'

'She just doesn't know you. Mom's a bit hair-trigger, if you know what I mean. What about your mom?'

'That little girl? Well, she was sweet, but now she wants to send me to the zoo ...' Roly-Poly choked back a rhino sob.

'It's okay, kiddo, I'm with you,' Rumble-Tumble said, nudging her gently. 'I'll look after you.'

'Thank you,' Roly-Poly squeaked. 'You're sweet.' She couldn't really believe her little girl had betrayed her like this.

'Let's have a snack and move on.' Rumble-Tumble heaved himself out of the mud, followed by Roly-Poly. 'Actually, I could do with a drink of milk,' he muttered, but had to settle for tussocks of grass. They fed for a while and then Roly-Poly said, 'Let's go—lead the way!'

Rumble-Tumble looked around. 'Ah, yes, that's the path we came by,' he said, trotting off towards an animal track leading away from the waterhole.

It wasn't, and all too soon the little rhinos realized that they were lost.

'Is there anyone we can ask for directions?' Roly-Poly said, looking around. But the forest seemed empty.

'Hey, look, those guys have seen us. They're coming down to help,' Rumble-Tumble said, looking skywards. Two huge shadows passed over them and then two massive vultures landed nearby.

'Well, well, well! What do we have here? Two baby rhinos all on their own! Where are your mammas, babies?' one of the vultures asked.

'We've run away,' Rumble-Tumble said. 'Do you know the way to Hyacinth bheel, sir?'

'Hyacinth bheel? But of course! And who may you sweet little things be?'

The baby rhinos introduced themselves.

'My good self is Lord Cult, and my good partner there is Lady Vult. Together we're known as the Culture Vultures.'

'Good to meet you, sir and ma'am. Could you show us the way?'

'Certainly! Just follow us.' The two huge birds hopped and skipped grotesquely, then took off with clumsy wing-beats. They gained height, circled and then set off westwards—opposite the direction of the Hyacinth bheel.

'We take 'em to the ravines and make 'em fall,' Lord Cult gloated, flicking a massive pinion. 'Then we can have 'em all to ourselves. Two fat juicy pumpkins!'

But they weren't the only creatures interested in the baby rhinos. Baghbahadur had put his nose to the ground and followed the babies, right up to the waterhole. Here he lost their scent as they had squelched about in the muddy water so much. Suddenly he froze. Something was approaching the waterhole. He crouched low, virtually invisible in the high grass as a gang of four hyenas loped up in single file, giggling hideously.

'Those vultures landed just beyond—they must have seen something, or something's lying dead there ready for the picking,' the leader said. 'They took off again … Come on, guys, let's follow them!'

The animals lurched off into the grass and Baghbahadur followed stealthily. Up ahead, the two baby rhinos were having a tough time running through the jungle while trying to follow the vultures.

High in the sky, Lord Cult had also noticed the hyenas.

'We're being followed! Those filthy dogs down there are looking up and following us. They know we're onto something.'

'And there's that ruddy tiger too, tracking the hyenas … bloody hell, this is a procession.' Before they could plan their next move, a massive flotilla of clouds engulfed them. Now, neither could they see the ground below nor could any animal on the ground see them.

Up ahead, Roly-Poly looked up and gasped. The sky was covered by clouds and there was no sign of Lord Cult or Lady Vult.

'They've vanished.' Roly-Poly wailed, looking around fearfully. There was a rustle in the grass and the baby rhinos squealed and backed off fearfully.

'It'ssss all right, babiessss! But what are you doing here? Are you lossst?' A python, as thick as a sumo-wrestler's thigh, eased out of the grass, its tongue flicking, its beady eyes on the rhino babies. 'May I introduce myself to you, my dears? Madame Squeezy, at your service.'

'Good afternoon, ma'am …' Rumble-Tumble stuttered. 'Er … we are on our way to Hyacinth bheel. Would you know in which direction that is?'

'Sausage rolls …' Madame Squeezy murmured absent-mindedly, her tongue flicking madly. She then smiled (if you can imagine that). 'What a coincidence, my dears—I was heading that way myself. It's where I usually spend my summer holidays. Just follow me!'

It was certainly easier following the big python than looking up at the sky and trying to follow the vultures. Besides, they had now entered a thick patch of forest with a canopy that all but hid the sky, which anyway was still cloudy.

Madame Squeezy indeed was heading towards the Hyacinth bheel. She had eaten about a fortnight ago, so wasn't very hungry at the moment, but knew that in a while she would be peckish again. And now she was taking her 'tiffin' along with her and it would last her at least six months. Two juicy sausage-roll baby rhinos! It was going to be a relaxing vacation. But it was beginning to get late and time to find shelter for the night.

'Tell you what,' Madame Squeezy said, 'there's a pond with a small island near here—we'll spend the night on it. It should be quite safe.'

So they did. They waded across in the twilight and then Madame Squeezy said softly, 'Babies, come closer. Here, let me cuddle you poor motherless little things.'

She wrapped her coils around the two rhino babies and jammed them together.

'How's that, babies? Feel better?'

'Er … ma'am, your coils are so cold …'

'What to do, dear, we're cold-blooded creatures. But you'll be safe within them!'

'Thank you, ma'am!'

The gang of hyenas and Baghbahadur had also lost track of the rhinos. First, the damn vultures had vanished in the clouds, and as they had blindly been following the flight path of the birds, they had not backed that up by following a scent trail on the ground. They gave up and Baghbahadur returned to his patrol, muttering evilly about a day wasted.

'Those stupid hyenas have nothing better to do than go on a wild goose chase all day,' he muttered. He wasn't too worried about the lost sausage rolls. The jungle had eyes and ears everywhere, and when they were spotted, word would spread pretty damn quickly. And he, being the prime predator, would be the first to be told and would have the first option to do what he wanted with them.

*

Back at Akash bheel and the SRPG HQ, it had been a completely dreadful afternoon for both Gaindaben and Teesta. Poor Gaindaben seemed to be on the verge of a nervous breakdown as she charged hither and thither searching for Rumble-Tumble. Irrationally, she accused poor Smiley Masi of gulping down her baba while she did yoga and then blamed innocent Sidhvi Gau Mataji for distracting her with her yoga lesson. Worried and unable to settle on the upset rhino's back for normal tick-removing operations, Angel Wing (who had delivered the secret messages back and forth between the lovers), flew off and apprised Sidhvi Gau Mataji of the situation.

'She's losing it!' he said gloomily. 'She's charging everything and everyone.'

'Shanti, bagulaji—I will go and see her!' the cow said, and, lowing and mooing, she set forth, a marigold garland (for sustenance) around her neck.

'You!' Gaindaben growled menacingly when the placid cow entered the meadow around the bheel.

'You're responsible for my baba going missing. You and your mumbo-jumbo-yoga-shoga-stick-your-left-leg-out-'n'-stick-your-right-leg-out-and-shake-it-all-about nonsense!'

'Shanti, puttari, shanti—peace, daughter, be peaceful!'

'How can I be at peace, you idiot? My baba is gone! Probably in that fat tiger's stomach by now and being burped up by him!'

'Khatta dakaar ho jaye—may he have acid reflux then,' Gau Mataji murmured. 'But I don't think so … did you scold him or forbid him from doing anything?'

'I scolded him all the time,' Gaindaben said with a sudden stifled snort. 'You know how kids are these days. He was running after that little hussy of a human-raised rhino baby all the time. I forbade him to do that!'

'Usse pyaar tha? Was he in love with her?'

'What! Are you nuts? He doesn't know the meaning of love! He is far too young for that sort of thing.'

'Aaj kal ke bachche—kids nowadays grow up very fast. I had a bachchada—a calf at my ashram that was in love with a gaur … they ran away together.' She shook her head. 'The gaur should have known better. He was old enough to be her grandfather—but they were really in love!'

'I don't care—I want my baba back!'

'Aa jayega—he'll come back to get your blessing. Be grateful he hasn't run away with a baby elephant!'

'What! Are you perverted or what?'

Sidhvi Gau Mataji lowered her voice. 'Bhenji, aap ne Animal Planet, Discovery ya National Geographic Channel dekha hai? My dear, have you watched Animal Planet, Discovery or National Geographic Channel? They show friendships between all sorts of creatures —parrots with bullmastiffs, goats with tigers, dogs and cats of course, cats and chickens—it is shameful. At least your baba is friends with another of his kind.'

'Will you stop lecturing and tell me how to get him back?'

'Shanti, betiji,' Gau Mataji lowered her voice. 'Er … did you speak to him about …' and she whispered in Gaindaben's ear. If Gaindaben could have blushed, she would have turned a deep plum.

'What? Are you crazy? What sort of ashram do you run? Of course my innocent baba knows nothing of that! Neither did his father, that big oaf—until he met me!'

'Naturally, he didn't know. He wasn't taught.'

'Madam, if you don't advise me on how to find my baby, I'm afraid I'm going to have to charge you!'

'Find the girl. You'll find your baba,' Sidhvi Gau Mataji inclined her graceful head and ate up her marigold garland. 'Now I have to chew the cud and meditate. You are welcome to join me.'

*

The downpour that had washed out the tracks of Roly-Poly and Baghbahadur from outside the enclosure was brief but heavy, and Teesta was frantic to start searching for her beloved little rhino. Commander Thapa and other SRPG staff had been informed and told to look out for her. The commander soon joined his upset little daughter.

'Don't worry, sweetheart, we'll find her,' he assured her, not feeling half as confident as he sounded. A baby rhino without its mother, out in the wilds, was a sitting duck. There were any number of predators which would make mincemeat out of her.

'Papa,' Teesta said suddenly, 'this morning that other baby rhino was missing too—Gaindaben's baby. She was so upset. Now Roly-Poly's gone too. Is someone kidnapping baby rhinos from here, and from under our noses?'

'You have a point, darling,' the commander frowned. He didn't like the way things were going. Was there a gang taking baby rhinos to sell to zoos? And doing so in broad daylight? From a place as prominent as Akash bheel and the SRPG HQ at that! It seemed improbable. Teesta called the prince.

'Shammy, Roly-Poly's run away!' Teesta cried. 'And that other little rascal is also missing.' Then her eyes grew large as dinner plates. 'Of course, they must have run away together!'

'What?'

'Yes, and we have to find them before that tiger gets them—he's after them!'

9

The little island where Madame Squeezy had taken her two little 'tiffins' was also the refuge of the Vindaloo Babes and their parents: every evening they came here to sleep. They had found a cosy rocky overhang, almost like a cave, where they cuddled together in one big heap and slept, while their parents dozed outside, grunting, alert for danger.

They were in for a shock that evening. As the Vindaloo Babes scampered up to the entrance, they skidded to a halt, and squealed.

'Oh my God, just look at that!'

'Gross!'

'She's got them both in her coils!'

'She's marinating them!'

'We have to do something!'

The hirsute Mamma Vindaloo trotted up and took in the scene.

'Babies, move away,' she grunted. 'We'll find another place for tonight.'

Madame Squeezy eyed the piglets greedily. Were two in hand worth twelve in the bush, she wondered? She'd been eyeing these piglets ever since they had been born—after all, they were the original sausage rolls. Papa Vindaloo rolled up and snorted angrily.

'Madam, kindly vacate this place. We have taken this cave on long lease. You are trespassing!'

'Ssssez whoooo?' Madame Squeezy hissed, her beady eyes unblinking.

'I do!' Papa Vindaloo snorted, smoke issuing from his nostrils. 'On the count of three.'

'You kids, wake up, get out of there. She's going to squeeze you to death,' the Vindaloo Babes shrilled at Roly-Poly and Rumble-Tumble. Daringly, they feinted towards the great snake, who struck at them, her tongue flicking.

'Come and get your spareribs, fat lady!'

'Pork chops!'

'Hot dogs!'

'Ham 'n' bacon!'

'Succulent pork belly!'

'If you dare!'

'Nyah, nyah, nyah!'

Roly-Poly and Rumble-Tumble opened their eyes sleepily.

'What's going on?' Roly-Poly murmured, happy to feel Rumble-Tumble right beside her.

Again the intrepid little piglets bobbed and feinted towards the great snake, sneering and jeering at it.

'Just look at them go,' Papa Vindaloo said proudly. 'They'll teach that fat serpent a lesson.'

'Babies, be careful!' Mamma Vindaloo warned. She was ready to charge, if the need arose. At the moment, the babies seemed to have matters well under control. The serpent had begun hissing with rage. Her movements were a bit handicapped because her great coils were still around her two tiffin rhinos and she had to be careful not to squeeze them too hard—just yet.

The Vindaloo Babes were getting bolder. One of them, quickly followed by the others, actually dared to poke her sharp little hooves into Madame Squeezy's polished coils.

'Get out of there, you morons!' one of the Babes yelled at the rhinos. 'Wriggle out.'

'Can't! We're a bit squashed,' Roly-Poly panted, suddenly feeling claustrophobic.

Madame Squeezy's icy eyes turned towards her and shimmered. 'It's okay, babies, don't be scared. I'll take care of those piglets. Now you stay right here while I deal with them!' She uncoiled herself from the rhinos and slithered after the piglets, hissing malevolently and striking out left and right.

'Vindaloos vamoose!' shrieked one of the Babes, and they scattered in different directions like a bomb exploding. Roly-Poly and Rumble-Tumble, stiff and cramped after being squashed together for so long, tottered out of the cave. Mamma Vindaloo came up to them, whisking her curly tail briskly.

'Come on, babies,' she said kindly, 'follow us.'

'B … but … the others?' Roly-Poly asked, looking around. 'Where have they gone?'

'They'll be fine; they know what to do.'

'And Madame Squeezy?' Rumble-Tumble asked.

'She wanted to swallow you, sweetie! Like she's wanted to swallow the Babes ever since they were born. Never trust a python, darling. Now come along!'

'You must be careful of the company you keep,' Papa Vindaloo grunted, digging up a tuber. 'Now, where have those bad girls of mine gone?'

'Here we are, Papa!' One by one the Vindaloo Babes popped out of the bushes, grinning, and kissed his hairy cheek (if you can imagine wild boars doing that). 'Okay babies, line up for a headcount!'

'And where have you left the good Madame Squeezy?' their mother inquired.

The Babes giggled. 'Oh, Madame Squeezy! She's in such a tizzy! She doesn't know what to do because we made her dizzy!'

Another Babe continued, 'She didn't know which one of us to chase. She'd chase Folly and then Lolly darted at her, then she went after Lolly and Dolly darted at her, and then she came after Dolly and Polly darted at her …'

'Okay, okay, we get the idea. Well done, chicklets.'

'In the end, she tied herself up into such a knot, it'll take her a month to undo herself!'

'She was fizzing like a geyser about to go up!'

'So where are you kids headed?' Mamma Vindaloo asked Roly-Poly. 'And what were you doing in Madame Squeezy's embrace?'

'We want to go to Hyacinth bheel, ma'am,' Rumble-Tumble said. 'She said she'd take us there.'

'Hey, we just spent some time at Hyacinth bheel teasing that fat dada rhino everyone calls Hulla,' one of the Babes chimed in. 'We had such fun! He pretends to be such a grouch.'

'Hulla? He's my dad,' Rumble-Tumble said proudly.

'Oh, we're sorry … we didn't mean to call him fat …'

'It's okay, my mom calls him much worse names. You mean he's at Hyacinth bheel?'

'Yes.'

'It's our most favourite place in the whole world.'

'We'll be going back there tomorrow.'

'Can we come along with you, please?'

'Our pleasure!'

Mamma Vindaloo eyed the two little rhinos keenly.

'Do your mothers know where you are?' she asked.

Roly-Poly and Rumble-Tumble exchanged glances. They knew they had no choice but to explain their position and hope for the best, so they did.

Mamma Vindaloo was a very pragmatic soul who had brought up many litters of feisty and fiercely independent piglets. Children were children, it didn't matter what species they were. Forbid them from doing something and that is exactly what they'd do. 'All right,' she said, 'we'll send word to Gaindaben that you are safe and happy, but won't tell her where you are. And we'll do the same to that smelly old goat who was babysitting you, dear: he can tell your little girl the same thing. Is that all right by you both?'

'Thank you, aunty,' the two baby rhinos chimed, their eyes shining.

'Now come on, kids, we'd better cross over quickly. It's getting dark and that python is still somewhere here.'

So they crossed over and took refuge under a gigantic banyan where they snuggled up and slept. Ever protective of them, the piglets formed a tight circle around the baby rhinos.

Unbeknownst to them, a massive search had got underway at first light the next morning. While most of the SRPG elephants had to remain with their rhino charges, Maharani, Hira and Rajkumari were pressed into service along with several Forest Department Gypsies and Jeeps and trackers on foot. But what was worse was that Baghbahadur and the hyena gang were hot on their trail once again. Baghbahadur, who had been shadowed by the hyenas (who now wanted to steal whatever he took down) had, during the course of his dawn patrol, caught a strong, if peculiar, whiff of python mixed with rhino and piglet. It had led him to the edge of the pond—and looming up ahead in the middle of the water stood the island.

On the island, what Baghbahadur confronted was a furious and still hopelessly knotted up Madame Squeezy. The strong and delicious aroma of tender pork cheeks and baby rhino burgers still drifted in the air.

'What the heck happened to you?' he growled, drooling at a respectable distance. He didn't trust Madame Squeezy one bit, and she really was throwing a hissy fit. 'Are you doing yoga too? That weird cow got inside your head as well? Everyone's doing yoga in this godforsaken jungle!'

'Shut up!' hissed the furious snake. 'Let me focussss!'

'What the heck is she doing?' one of the hyenas giggled as they shoved each other and wagged their tails.

'Get out of here, you dirtbags!' Baghbahadur growled, sending the hyenas into fresh paroxysms of giggles. They were staring, as if hypnotized, at the great snake, whose coils were shimmering and shivering as she untied herself knot by knot.

'Are you playing cat's cradle with yourself?' one of the hyenas asked, and they all fell about giggling hideously. 'Careful you don't strangle and swallow yourself!'

'Where are the rhinos and piglets?' Baghbahadur asked, looking around. 'The whole place is redolent with them! They must have been here.'

'Those rhino babies are mine!' hissed Madame Squeezy. 'But they've gone. Those wretched piglets tricked me into tying myself up, and took off.' And then suddenly, the last knot in her coils came undone and she was free. Both Baghbahadur and the hyenas sprang back several feet and watched warily.

'Right,' Madame Squeezy said, stretching herself to her full fifteen feet. 'We follow them. We catch them. I take the rhinos, you can have the piglets and their parents.'

'What about us?' the hyenas snickered.

'Leftovers, if any,' growled Baghbahadur. He eyed the giant snake. Of course, he wasn't going to let her swallow both the baby rhinos while he went helter-skelter after those piglets. Let the hyenas run after them. He'd go for the mamma lode, the python herself—while she constricted the rhino babies and softened them up. What a kill that would be!

'Let's go!' he growled as the python slithered sinuously past, her tongue flicking as she caught the scent.

'Tally-ho!' shrieked the hyenas, keeping a safe distance from the tiger, and loping along in their hunched, hangdog manner.

*

At the SRPG HQ, the search strategy had been drawn out early that morning.

'We'll check all the bheels systematically first,' Commander Thapa said. 'They're sure to be at one of them. Rhinos can't do without them.' He smiled encouragingly at an anxious Teesta. 'We'll find her, sweetheart. Probably some SRPG ranger will spot the rascals soon.'

'I hope so,' Teesta said sadly. 'I hope we find them before those poachers or a tiger does.' She looked at her father. 'Can I ask Prince Shammy to come along with us? It'll be useful for his school project.'

'Okay, if the maharaja and maharani have no objection.'

The prince was thrilled to be included in the search. Rosy and Posy too insisted that they come along and their parents agreed, glad to have the girls out of their hair.

'I hope we find them soon,' Prince Shammy told Teesta. 'What do we do after we find them?'

Teesta's face fell. 'We'll have to tranquilize them and take the ruffian back to his mother and ... and

Roly-Poly to the zoo, like your parents ordered.' She looked at him pleadingly. 'Can't you make them change their minds? You said you would! You know how sweet Roly-Poly is.'

Prince Shammy nodded seriously. 'Don't worry, Teesta. I told you, I've thought of something. A plan. I can't tell you what it is, but once I execute it, Papa and Mamma will have no choice but to let Roly-Poly go free. I promise!'

'What? You have a secret plan? You *promise* to free Roly-Poly?' She could hardly believe it. He was a prince; he would keep his word.

'Yes,' he said solemnly. 'It is a dangerous plan, but it will work. It has to!' He gulped. 'If you like, you can even come along when I execute it, but you must promise not to interfere in any way.'

'I love you, I love you, I love you!' Teesta flung her arms around him and kissed him four times on each cheek.

'Woo-hoo!' Rosy and Posy squealed, clapping in delight. 'She loves you, Shammy!'

'Do you promise to not interfere?' the prince asked, still regally solemn and a little pink. Her lips had felt so soft, like rose petals.

'I do! I won't interfere.' Her eyes shone.

*

'Safe? What do you mean he's safe and happy? He's not here with me! How can he be safe and happy?' Gaindaben tossed her head angrily as the egret that had just landed on her back flew off with a squawk of protest.

'Ma'am, I'm just the courier. This was the message I was told to deliver to you.'

'By who?'

'That's classified, ma'am. It'll be declassified in thirty years. You'll know then.'

'How can he be safe and happy without his mamma?'

'Maybe because your baba is growing up,' the egret muttered under his breath.

'What did you say?' the furious rhino mom demanded. 'This is all the fault of that fat oaf Hulla! If he had been a proper father, none of this would have happened.'

'True, ma'am,' the egret said solemnly, landing on Gaindaben's back again and snapping up a juicy tick.

'It's time that fat oaf took some responsibility for his actions,' Gaindaben snorted. 'Do you know where he is?'

'Yes, ma'am. At Hyacinth bheel, ma'am, and frolicking with some whistling teals, according to the grapevine.'

'What? I'll show him what frolicking is! He'd better start looking for his only son and heir or I'm going to toss him into the river.' She hauled her great bulk out of Akash bheel and set off at a lumbering rolling trot towards Hyacinth bheel.

*

Madame Squeezy, Baghbahadur and the hyena gang too were making swift progress following the pungent scent of the piglets and rhinos. Madame Squeezy slithered through the jungle as Baghbahadur bounded after her and the hyenas brought up the rear, with their easy loping stride. Up in the heavens, Lady Vult and Lord Cult spotted them again and were disappointed. A python, a tiger and hyenas, all after the rhino babies and piglets—there wouldn't be many leftovers from this kill.

'Foiled again!' Lord Cult muttered as Lady Vult flew alongside.

'See no reason why we shouldn't spoil their party, though,' Lady Vult said, blinking her beady eyes.

'What do you mean?'

'We'll whistle up the others and go down low after them. Those rangers in their jeeps and elephants will follow us and be onto them in no time at all, like bluebottles on a kill. There goes the party. And then we'll do the Ghouls' Dance to celebrate!'

*

Completely unaware that they were being followed, the Vindaloo family and baby rhinos rolled through the jungle, snorting happily. Roly-Poly gently butted Rumble-Tumble. 'Hey, have you thought of what we're going to do when we reach Hyacinth bheel? I mean your dad is there … What if he throws us out?'

'We'll have to find another place, I guess. But I hope he won't.' Rumble-Tumble sounded doubtful.

'Have you actually met him?' Roly-Poly asked him. 'I mean, does he even know he has a son?'

'Ya, ya, he knows! He even came to see me, but Mamma wouldn't let him come anywhere near me. Said she didn't want me to come under his "bad influence".'

'Oh, well, I guess if it doesn't work out with your dad, we can always go to the Chhoti Talao, though it is a bit too close to the road … But it'll be perfect for us, just our size! No adult animal will interfere with us there.'

'I need a good long wallow right now!' Rumble-Tumble grumbled.

*

The SRPG search party had just scoured the area around Akash bheel and begun making their way towards Hyacinth bheel, their next port of call. To their surprise, Gaindaben was not to be seen at Akash bheel, which had been her favourite haunt for so many days.

'Now where's she disappeared?' Teesta wondered, and Commander Thapa began getting uncomfortable butterflies in his stomach. But then he got a message from the ranger deputed to Gaindaben and who had been dutifully following her.

'She's rolling along at quite a clip ... seems to be heading towards Hyacinth bheel, over!'

'Keep us informed. We're heading that way too.' The ranger deputed to Hulla had reported that the rhino had yet again started off towards the bridge.

'It looks like he wants to go across into the fields again.'

'Try and stop him!'

'Will be difficult, sir. The bridge won't hold the weight of my elephant, and the river has risen. It'll be dangerous to ford it. The current is very strong.'

Hulla indeed had been contemplating another foray into the fields across the bridge. It would certainly liven up the day. He snorted at the ranger's elephant, swivelled around and rumbled over the ominously creaking bridge, even as the waters swirled inches beneath the planks. Behind him, the ranger on the elephant yelled himself hoarse, to no avail, and the elephant trumpeted her frustration. This time she knew she couldn't cross the river.

'Papa, maybe Gaindaben is following Rumble-Tumble's spoor,' Teesta said hopefully. 'Why should she want to leave Akash bheel otherwise? Maybe that ruffian fellow has gone looking for his dad.'

'We'll soon know,' the commander said. He asked the ranger deputed to Hulla if he had seen any baby rhinos around.

'Nahin sahib—no sir, but Hulla has gone across to the village again and I can't follow on my elephant because the river is too high.'

'Follow him on foot then. We should be there in a little while and will give you backup. He mustn't destroy their crops.'

'Very well, sir.'

'Looks like we're going to have to round up that rogue Hulla before we can look for Roly-Poly,' the commander told Teesta and the children. 'He can wreak havoc in no time at all.'

'Oh my God,' Teesta said suddenly, 'if Gaindaben gets there and finds Roly-Poly with Rumble-Tumble, she'll charge her!'

'Baby, we'll take each crisis as it comes,' said her father, hugging her lightly. 'No point worrying about it now.'

*

Roly-Poly, Rumble-Tumble and the Vindaloo Babes (and their parents) were the first to reach Hyacinth bheel. It was deserted and tethered near the bridge, the ranger's elephant grazed quietly. The piglets approached the bheel cautiously and finding that the coast seemed clear (except for the happy-go-lucky whistling teals), went berserk, racing and chasing each other, scratching their bottoms on rocks, wallowing blissfully. Their happy mood infected their parents—and the little rhinos—and before long, it was a happy bedlam at Hyacinth bheel.

And then, through the tall elephant grass, Madame Squeezy slithered out, followed by Baghbahadur and the hyenas a little distance away. High above, a squadron of around fifteen vultures circled over them, gradually losing height. Madame Squeezy took in the scene and retreated into the grass, with only her head poking out. The baby rhinos would tire soon enough and lie down in the mud—that's when she would strike. This time she would finish the job, the efforts of untangling herself, and the chase had made her hungry again. Behind her, unseen, Baghbahadur crouched, his tail lashing like a lariat as he waited for the python to make her move. A thought suddenly struck him and he licked his chops. The piglets too would soon tire and lie down to feed against their mother's tummy—that's when he'd go for them. Once Madame Squeezy had committed herself to constricting and swallowing the rhinos, she would be unable to go anywhere—easy meat, hah-hah! So the piglets would be his appetizers and the python and baby rhinos his main course. A fitting feast for an alpha male tiger!

*

'What's Hulla up to?' the commander radioed the ranger who had been shadowing the rhino.

'Sir, he has rolled into the village and … and, um, seems to have fallen asleep in front of a cow!' There was reverence in the man's voice.

'What!'

'He's lying prostrate in front of this black and white cow who is sitting in the middle of the road, as all cows do, chewing cud.'

'Is he breathing?'

'Yes.'

Hulla was, in fact, receiving wisdom at the feet of Sidhvi Gau Mataji.

'Khamosh, puttar—quiet, son,' Gau Mataji said softly. 'Cleanse your mind of all unpleasant, unclean thoughts.'

Hulla promptly thought of all the great times he had had with Gaindaben, before he'd said something rude to rile her.

'The last time we met, she really showed me,' he said. 'I fear she may have dumped me.'

'What did you say to her to make her angry?'

'Nothing! Only that I knew she couldn't live without me, the biggest, most handsome rhino in the world, and would pine forever if I left her, and it was my right to flirt and go with as many girls as I wished.'

'Hmm …'

'Don't know why, but it made her mad. Can you tell me why?'

'Puttar, what if she told you she was seeing other rhino fellows besides you?'

Hulla erupted, snorting and bellowing. 'I'd trample them and toss them into the river! Has she told you that?' He was so incensed, he charged a handcart and upset it. He pawed the ground and lowered his head at the nearest hut (behind which, the villagers were watching, entranced and now terrified), determined to flatten it.

'Khamosh, puttar!' Gau Mataji said. 'You must not excite yourself so. It is bad for your blood pressure. Do you know Gaindabenji is very upset at the moment? You need to go and comfort her.'

'Upset? Why? Is she missing me? I knew it!'

'Her little baba has gone missing.'

'What?'

'He is so like you,' Gau Mataji said, her sloe eyes shrewd. 'I think he gave his heart to a little girl rhino and ran after her. He's taken just after his father, I think ...'

'What? That little runt? He's already chasing chicklets?' There was a note of pride in the big rhino's gruff voice.

'Children these days! What to do? They pick up all sorts of things from National Geographic and Discovery channels.'

'So what can I do?'

'Simple. If you find her baba, and take him back to her, she'd be eternally grateful to you.'

'Find the little runt? He could be coochie-smooching anywhere!'

Gau Mataji closed her eyes. 'Beta, if you were him, where would you take your little sweetheart?'

A strong gust of cool, monsoon breeze blew over from the sanctuary and wound its way through the village, scooping up leaves and twigs, and making the puddles ripple. Hulla suddenly sniffed and snorted and swivelled around, his nose and ears twitching madly.

'She's here! Gaindaben's here! She's wearing that perfume I cannot resist. I must go!' And without so much as a by your leave, he rumbled through the village back towards the bridge, surprising the ranger and making him dive into the bushes to get out of the way in time.

*

At the Hyacinth bheel, Gaindaben had finally arrived and was grimly assessing the situation. Out there, in the shallows, her baba was shamelessly cavorting with his disreputable girlfriend, in the midst of a sounder of wild boar piglets! Could there be anything more shameful and distressing for a mamma rhino to witness? She had a good mind to just abandon him. Kids these days were just so ungrateful and thought they knew everything. She heard a snort behind her and swivelled around. Hulla was standing there, looking at her in that way which made her massive knees go all wobbly.

'What do you want?' she asked as coldly as she could.

'Look at him!' Hulla snorted proudly. 'Our son! Already a little man! They sure grow up fast these days, don't they?'

'Certainly faster than you ever did,' Gaindaben responded tartly. 'And it's all your fault that he's chasing skirts at such a young age.'

'Can't help it if he's got my good looks and charisma and is a chicklet-magnet, can I? None of the gals can resist that!'

'Good looks? Charisma? Pah!' Gaindaben snorted, tossing her head. Her knees were quivering like jelly as Hulla came and stood beside her. What a guy he was; his armour plating impervious to everything and, alas, his heart seemed to be equally impervious …

'Say, you okay?' he asked, eyeing her. 'You're a bit wobbly on your pins.'

'Don't you dare call my magnificent thunder thighs pins,' she snapped.

'You know, that yogic cow woman in the village said I might have said or done something to upset you. I don't know what that could possibly be, but whatever it is—or you imagined it to be—I'm sorry! Didn't mean to hurt your feelings and whatnot.'

Gaindaben nearly fainted. He, the gross, insensitive, impervious Hulla, had actually apologized.

'It's … it's okay …' she stuttered faintly, not realizing that she was leaning against him now. 'It's just that I'm a little upset with our little roadside Romeo there. Carrying on with that human-raised hussy. He's too good for her!'

'Would you like me to go in and break it up?' he asked.

Before she could answer, things began happening very quickly indeed.

Madame Squeezy had decided on her strategy with diabolical cunning: she would attack the little boy rhino first and wrap her coils around him. Girls, being more faithful than guys, would recklessly come to his rescue … and then she'd throw her massive coils around her too! The piglets would scatter in the commotion and the tiger could chase them all he liked. She slithered towards Rumble-Tumble who was lying in a comfortable wallow just vacated by Mamma Vindaloo, his eyes closed in bliss. Roly-Poly was scratching her bottom against a rock, also, alas, with her eyes closed. The Vindaloo Babes had made their mom lie down again and open her milk bar. Papa Vindaloo was dozing.

'Hello, little boy, we meet again!' Madame Squeezy hissed as she launched herself at Rumble-Tumble, sliding over the mud towards him at high speed.

'Whaa...?' he squawked, trying to get to his feet in a hurry and slipping in the slick mud. Before he knew it, the great snake was trying to lash her coils around him. But the little rhino was covered with slick, slippery mud and he slid right through her coils before she could tighten them around him. 'Help!' Rumble-Tumble squawked, unbalanced and rolling upside down, 'Help me!' As he floundered, trying to get out of the muddy wallow, Madame Squeezy readied herself for a second launch. This time there would be no mistake.

Roly-Poly didn't hesitate for a second. 'Leave him alone, you big bully!' she screamed as she charged the surprised python and stomped and bounced heavily all over her, butting her as hard as she could with her tough little head.

'Ooof, my back!' Madame Squeezy yelped. 'You've put my back out!' Roly-Poly landed heavily on the back of her neck, making her writhe and wriggle, like a giant earthworm on a hook. 'Ouch—my neck ... okay, that's enough!'

The Vindaloo Babes shot up from feeding as Mamma Vindaloo jerked up and Papa Vindaloo awoke. Baghbahadur, who had just been about to pounce on them, crouched back with a frustrated growl. Again, he'd missed his chance!

'What the ...?' Papa Vindaloo shouted.

At the edge of the elephant grass, Gaindaben and Hulla watched, transfixed.

'Oh my God!' Hulla said, disgusted. 'My son, rescued by a mere chit of a girl! What is the world coming to these days?'

Also at the edge of the elephant grass, Baghbahadur watched, getting more and more confused by the moment. Now who should he attack? Madame Squeezy had failed to take down the rhinos and was writhing about, moaning about her back and neck; the rhino babies were scrambling out of the water and the piglets were scampering up and down the banks of the bheel, squealing, while their parents bristled and snorted, checking for danger. He crouched, belly low to the ground, as Roly-Poly and Rumble-Tumble scampered out of the bheel, panting with fright and rolling their eyes.

'Thanks!' Rumble-Tumble stuttered, still in a state of shock. 'I thought she had got me!'

'Not on my watch!' Roly-Poly said in a quivering voice. 'But we'd better get out of here fast!' Instinctively, she had moved towards the high elephant grass, very close to where Baghbahadur crouched. His eyes gleamed and his tail twitched excitedly. This time he would not miss his chance! But then his tail twitch was spotted.

'Tiger!' snorted Gaindaben, and charged, giving poor Roly-Poly the fright of her life.

'Your mom, she really has got it in for me!' she squealed, scampering out of the way as the enraged rhino-mom seemed to be headed straight for her. 'She really hates me!' But then, Gaindaben veered off straight into the high grass and Roly-Poly saw the flash of flame and black as Baghbahadur turned and fled with a frustrated growl, nearly running headlong into the hyenas who scuttled away giggling.

High above, Lord Cult and Lady Vult turned their beaks up in disgust. 'Oh crap! They've messed up again, abort mission. No kills here!' they radioed and veered off.

'Dd … did you see that?' Roly-Poly stuttered as she nearly fell against Rumble-Tumble. 'There was a tiger there, crouched and ready to pounce on me!'

'Ya … ya …' Rumble-Tumble said, hardly comprehending what had happened. Things were happening just too fast. Roly-Poly's eyes were shining.

'Your mom … she saved me,' she said, nuzzling Rumble-Tumble. 'She must love me!'

And then Gaindaben stood there in front of them, snorting, her flanks heaving. 'Young man, you are in more trouble than you will ever know. Now come with me at once or your father will have something to say about this!' She looked around for old Hulla and snorted in disgust. Hulla was playing tag with the Vindaloo Babes, chasing them into the bheel and being chased by them, snorting and roaring with mock rage. For the rhino with the baddest temper in the Gaindagunj National Park, it looked like he really was a big softie when it came to kids!

Sitting stupefied on their elephants, Teesta, Prince Shamsher, the commander, Rosy, Posy and the others watched the scene unfold before them in amazement. Nothing like this had been witnessed before in the history of the park. Then, at last, it was time for order to be re-established.

'Rumble-Tumble, come on now, we have to go home,' Gaindaben ordered imperiously. It was clear that Roly-Poly had not been invited to accompany them.

'Roly-Poly! Baby, come here, baby, chocolate digestive biscuits,' Teesta said in her magic voice, slipping down Maharani's broad back before her father could object. 'I was so worried about you!' She ran up to the little rhino and hugged her.

The two little rhinos looked at each other for a long moment, then turned and followed their moms.

Up on Maharani, Prince Shamsher looked at Hulla, standing there, waist deep in the bheel, his flanks heaving as the piglets were led off into the jungle by their parents, their tails up like antennae.

'Thanks, uncle!' they squealed. 'We had great fun. We'll come again tomorrow to play with you.'

Hmm, the prince thought, the fellow was a fool. He'd be easy to kill.

'Now, Roly-Poly, please follow Maharani and Hira back home,' Teesta said earnestly, even though her little heart was sinking. All too soon, her beloved little rhino would be dispatched to Gaindagunj zoo, and that would be that.

Unless, Prince Shammy kept his promise to her. Back up on Maharani's broad back and sitting next to him, she leant over and whispered, 'Her fate is now in your hands.'

He nodded, his face expressionless, his hand clutching hers hard.

10

'Tonight, Your Highness, we will conduct the tarpan tonight. The full moon rises early. We should leave the palace by around 9 pm and be at the bheel in half an hour. We locate the rhino and you shoot him. And then …' Mutthiji gloated, 'all will be well ever after.'

'Mutthiji, as I told you earlier, I want Teesta to come with us, to witness the ceremony.'

'Her parents may not permit her to leave home at that hour.'

'Arrange it, Mutthiji, so that they do. She must come along with us!'

'Very well, huzoor. I will send the commander a fake tip about the location of poachers, so he will go after them; and shall arrange for something to be slipped into the madam's dinner so that she sleeps very soundly.'

'Whatever! Just do it!'

'Consider it done!'

'Tonight?' Teesta's eyes glowed with excitement. 'And you've arranged that Papa and Mamma won't know I'm not at home? Wow! I love you!'

'Be ready at eight thirty sharp, and wear dark clothes.'

'And you're still not going to tell me what it's all about?'

'No, I can't. It has to be a secret till the end. And by the way, we'll have to blindfold you on the way. So don't mind that.'

'What?' It was becoming more exciting by the second.

'Ya, you must never know where we're going. You will only be allowed to see what you have to see, and nothing more. Those are the conditions!'

'Shammy!' Teesta was thrilled. 'Wow! I can hardly wait!'

*

At the Akash bheel, Rumble-Tumble had just helped himself to a refreshing 30 litres of milk and was arguing with his mother.

'Mamma, you saw what she did. She saved me from that python. She just charged at her and stomped on her!'

'Humph, I didn't see anything of the sort,' Gaindaben fibbed, turning broadside.

'Ask Papa, he'll tell you,' Rumble-Tumble said. 'He was there right beside you!'

'Your papa is the most unreliable rhino in the world,' Gaindaben said again, not very convincingly. 'Now why don't you go to sleep? You've had a long day.'

'Mamma, you must like her,' Rumble-Tumble cried, and then played his ace. 'I mean, you rescued Roly-Poly from that tiger just as he was about to pounce on her. You charged him and drove him away! Why did you do that?'

'Umm ... umm ...' Gaindaben really didn't understand what had made her come to that pestiferous little rhino's rescue. 'You ... you know, I'm short-sighted—I thought she was you.'

'What!' Rumble-Tumble was outraged. 'No way. I'm not buying that!'

And then Gaindaben realized why she had rescued little Roly-Poly. The little rhino reminded her of herself: feisty and always ready to protect the one she loved, no matter what the risk. If the little rhino had come to the rescue of her Rumble-Tumble, putting her own life in danger, she must love the little runt a lot. It did hurt her to realize that there was another rhino who cared about her baba as much (if not more) as she did—but that made him a very lucky little baba. It was not something she ought to be objecting to.

'Okay,' she agreed at last, 'if she comes here again, you may play with her. I don't mind. Actually, she's quite sweet.'

Rumble-Tumble was happy and sad at the same time. It was all very well for his mamma to say this now, knowing that Roly-Poly would probably never come to Akash bheel again. He would never see her again.

*

At seven thirty that evening, Mutthiji entered Prince Shamsher's chambers holding the beautiful old Winchester rifle in his hand.

'This is the gun you shall use, Your Highness,' he said. 'It's the same gun your daduji used.'

It was heavy, but Prince Shammy held it to his shoulder gamely and squinted down the barrel.

'I will load it when we get to the bheel,' Mutthiji told him, 'with a single heavy calibre bullet that will take the beast down instantly. I will provide backup in case it's needed, so you need not worry about anything. I will also give you a clip of six extra cartridges. Better be safe than sorry!'

'Thank you, Mutthiji, I'm not worried,' the prince said, his eyes shining.

The khaki palace gypsy whispered into the SRPG HQ compound at ten minutes past nine, with its headlights doused. Sure enough, a call had been received by the commander at 8.30 p.m. There had been an urgent tip-off regarding poachers and he, along with Jawahar Singh, had set off on their elephants to investigate.

Teesta and her mother had their dinner by eight and by eight fifteen respectively; her mother had gone yawning to her bedroom to sleep. Teesta paced about impatiently in the verandah, waiting to be picked up.

'Sorry, but we have to do this,' Prince Shammy said, as he gently tied the black silk scarf around Teesta's eyes. 'I hope you don't mind.'

'Shammy, this is just so thrilling,' Teesta whispered. 'Are you sure it will work?'

'Yes!'

Teesta had been both a bit disappointed and a bit reassured when she saw that Mutthiji was with the prince. It would have been wonderful to have gone on this adventure alone with the prince, but an adult did provide some sort of backup support, in case things went wrong. What she hadn't seen was the Winchester rifle in its case, under the seat of the Gypsy, or the gleaming carving knives with which poor Hulla was to be carved up later.

They reached Hyacinth bheel at around 9.15 p.m. and Mutthiji parked the Gypsy at the head of the rhino pathway that led into the water. Up ahead was the big peepul tree under which Hulla did his business.

'Okay, Teesta baby, will you remain in the car while we make all the arrangements?' Mutthiji said in his soft whispery way. 'We should be back in ten minutes.'

'Okay, Mutthiji, but hurry, I'm dying to know what this is all about,' she said. 'I can smell water ... where are we? Near the river?'

'You'll know soon enough,' Mutthiji said, quietly retrieving the rifle from under the seat and handing it over to the prince. 'Now sit quietly and promise not to take the blindfold off, until we say so. We'll be back soon.'

'How do we know where to find Hulla?' the prince asked Mutthiji as the two of them set off.

'I received word that he should be near the big peepul tree. He likes that spot. He was reported there at 7.45 p.m., so he should still be there, or nearby.'

Old Hulla was, in fact, quite near the big peepul tree, grazing quietly and thinking about Gaindaben. Maybe he should go and look her up again. It was a lovely evening, the forest scented with wild herbs and other monsoon perfumes. He'd look like a medieval knight in shining armour—irresistible to any lady rhino, no matter how thick her hide.

A hundred metres away, Mutthiji gripped the prince's arm and stopped, and pointed silently at the great rhino.

Fortunately, the breeze was blowing from the rhino towards them, so Hulla didn't smell them. And both of them had trodden very softly indeed.

'Fetch Teesta!' Prince Shammy commanded in a whisper. 'She has to see what I do.'

In the Gypsy, Teesta had been unable to resist sliding the blindfold down and peeking. 'Oh,' she whispered to herself, blinking, 'we're at Hyacinth bheel again.' She had been here so many times, she could recognize the landmarks night or day. Then she spotted Mutthiji walking swiftly towards the car and hastily pushed the blindfold back up.

'Come along,' he said, taking her arm and guiding her along the path. 'The prince awaits you.'

He led her to the base of the big peepul tree and undid her blindfold. She blinked and looked around.

'Now climb the tree. Up to that branch … you'll be able to see everything from there. But be quiet. Everything will be explained later.'

She did as bidden and was soon sitting on a branch about 12 feet up, her legs dangling, looking down the jungle path. Then she stiffened. About 20 metres ahead, a small slight figure stood with his back to the tree. As she watched, she saw Mutthiji go up to the figure and whisper something. He then just seemed to melt away. The figure turned around—it was Prince Shammy! In one hand he held a rifle. He raised his other hand in greeting and then turned back. What the heck was going on? She was just about to call out to him, when some distance ahead of him, she saw movement. And from the shadows of the high elephant grass, the most gigantic rhino in the world stepped out into the bright moonlight.

Hulla had just made up his mind to go and look up Gaindaben.

The breeze was still blowing stiffly from him to the prince so he smelt nothing. He was short-sighted too, and didn't notice the still figure standing there. The prince made not a sound as he raised the heavy rifle to his shoulder and squinted down the sights. What he saw made his heart thump. A mighty animal, cast in glinting gunmetal armour, the rivets on its hide silver-bright in the moonlight; standing stock still, facing him, unafraid, lord of all he surveyed.

'He is going to shoot Hulla!' Teesta thought disbelievingly. She nearly squealed as the tree shook, and before she knew it, Mutthiji was sitting beside her. He balanced his rifle against the tree trunk and quickly clamped a hand over her mouth.

'No sound, Teesta baby. Let the prince perform the ceremony. He must kill the rhino.'

'Mmmmghf!'

'It is an ancient ceremony and all the rulers of Gaindagunj must carry it out. The prince's father failed to. So he must! He will kill the rhino and then we shall cut it open and he shall crawl into its belly and offer its blood as libation to the souls of his ancestors. He will be honoured in all Gaindagunj tomorrow!'

'Mmmmghfff!'

'Shh!' Deftly Mutthiji took the scarf they had used as a blindfold and expertly gagged Teesta. 'You have to remain silent!' he hissed. 'Or the prince will be in grave danger and you shall be blamed!'

Teesta shook her head wildly. This could not be happening! This was a nightmare. Worse than the night she had spent in the ditch with Roly-Poly! What the heck was wrong with Prince Shammy? Standing there in front of the baddest rhino in Gaindagunj, with a rifle at his shoulder? Any second now, the rhino would spot him and charge and pulp him right in front of her. Mutthiji was gripping her arm tightly, his eyes on the boy and the rhino.

Prince Shamsher held the heavy rifle to his shoulder as steadily as he could, and took aim. But then Hulla swivelled again and faced the other way. The prince waited. He didn't want to shoot the rhino with its back towards him, as it were. Then it turned around again and faced him, like that massive rhino had done with his daduji ...

And suddenly, it struck him! Could he really do it? Was it really necessary to pull the trigger and destroy something so truly monumental and magnificent? Shoot it, disembowel it and bathe in its blood? What would that prove? Surely he'd passed the test of courage by standing in front of the massive beast (no way any of the louts in his class would be able to do this), so what more did he need to prove? Sure, it would have been even more courageous if he'd stood there without the gun, unarmed … nevertheless … And even his dadiji had said that she hadn't been sure if Daduji's ancestors had achieved peace by the conducting of the ritual.

On the tree branch, Teesta suddenly went limp. Mutthiji stared at her in surprise and disgust—she had fainted! They should never have brought along the girl—trust her to faint at a crucial moment. He loosened his grip on her arm and shook her shoulders gently. Suddenly, she slithered from his grip and was climbing down the tree as swiftly as a gibbon. She yanked at the gag around her mouth, but it was too late.

Her crashing descent through the tree startled both Hulla and the prince. Both of them turned. Hulla saw the prince and the prince saw Teesta, now haring towards him, yanking at the gag across her face. Hulla rolled and rumbled straight for the prince. Teesta skimmed down the jungle path, her arms outstretched, eyes bulging.

'What the …!' the prince squawked, indicating like a traffic cop that Teesta should stop. 'Hold it!' Then he sensed the rumble behind him and turned around. Hulla was bearing down like a runaway tank at 40 kmph, grunting madly. Instinctively, the prince took aim and fired. The flash and blast startled Hulla but he just kept coming straight on. The kick of the rifle sent the prince flying backwards, straight into Teesta's outstretched arms as she raced towards him.

'Ooouf!'

'Oww!'

Dazed, they sat up in the path, stars spinning madly around them.

Up on the peepul tree, Mutthiji raised his rifle and waited. In a matter of seconds, the giant rhino would be all over the children, trampling them to death and ripping them to shreds with his incisors. Then, and only then, would he pull the trigger and give it the coup de grace! His plan was working perfectly—if Commander Thapa's little daughter was collateral damage, so be it. She was at the wrong place at the wrong time, that was all.

Teesta sat up in the mud and watched with horrified grapefruit eyes as Hulla thundered towards her and the prince, now perhaps just 10 metres away. Her arms were still clasped around the prince, who was moaning softly, semi-conscious, and shaking his head.

'Hulla, stop!' Teesta shrieked in panic. She grabbed the prince by the collar and yanked at him hard, rolling over to the side of the path, dragging him along, and falling into the muddy ditch running alongside, only in the nick of time. Hulla barrelled past them, tossing his head at empty air and then caught a fresh whiff of Mutthiji blowing down from the peepul tree—next to his precious dung heap! Up on the tree, Mutthiji blinked. A second ago, both children were about to be mowed down by the rhino, then suddenly they were gone and only the rhino remained, charging towards the tree at a hellish pace. Hulla rammed the tree so hard that Mutthiji lost his balance and crashed down headfirst, landing straight in the midden heap at its base. His rifle fell alongside him and discharged a round, the bullet whining harmlessly into the sky and this time, Hulla veered away and crashed on past the Gypsy along the path and vanished. He very badly needed to be comforted by Gaindaben tonight, make no mistake!

The children crawled out of the ditch, soaked and covered with mud. The water had revived the prince (who spat out an indignant tadpole) somewhat.

Teesta got to her feet and stood arms akimbo in front of him.

'Just why the heck were you trying to kill poor old Hulla?' she demanded. 'Are you sick in the head? All you maharaja types are wacko!'

'Th... the tar... tarpan,' he stuttered. 'Mutthiji said I must do it to save Papa and Daduji's souls. And ... and I wanted to impress you. So I agreed ...'

'What tarpan? Impress me? What for?'

'But ... but I shot Hulla and nothing happened to him ... He just kept charging ...' He was still rather dazed.

'Good for him!' Teesta retorted. 'Now explain!'

So he did as they slowly made their way to the base of the tree where Mutthiji lay in Hulla's dung heap, unconscious.

'I thought if I did it, Papa would be ashamed and not send me back to boarding school, and then I could ask them to let Roly-Poly remain in the sanctuary too and not be taken to the zoo.'

'So you were ready to kill old Hulla for that?' Teesta didn't know what to feel. She still very strongly felt like whacking the prince and also kissing him all over.

'But I missed,' the prince went on, sounding bewildered. 'I couldn't have missed from that distance! He was right in front of me. And nothing happened. He didn't even flinch!'

'Because he's a grand old rhino, that's why,' Teesta said. 'Maybe the bullet just bounced off him!'

'Between the eyes! I aimed between his eyes! He didn't even flinch and just kept coming. Like his father!'

'Well, hopefully, he's gone now and won't come back. We better go back too.' She looked up into the tree. 'Where's Mutthiji? He gagged me and told me to stay up there.'

'Hey, look at the base of the tree … he seems to have fallen down.'

The prince had picked up his rifle and stared at it disbelievingly. 'I just couldn't have missed,' he went on, 'my aim is very good.'

'Thank God, you did!'

In the muck, Mutthiji stirred. His mouth was full of something wet, squishy and very stinky. He groaned and sat up. The children stood near him, reluctant to help him out because he was covered with Hulla's dung.

'Are … are you all right, Mutthiji?' the prince asked at last. 'I … I appeared to have missed! Hulla's gone. What do we do now?'

Mutthiji cleared the muck out of his eyes and shook his head. 'We have to track him down and finish the job. You may have wounded him.'

The prince shook his head. 'I don't think so—he just went past us, and there's no blood trail … I missed completely!' Again, he looked disbelievingly at the rifle. 'I'd better reload it,' he said. He fished out a cartridge from his pocket and reloaded the rifle.

Mutthiji stumbled back to the Gypsy and began wiping himself down with a piece of cotton waste. That little girl had royally screwed up everything! And now the prince might be too scared to kill the rhino … his whole grand plan was unravelling. He would not allow that to happen. He retrieved his gun and reloaded it.

'Chalo huzoor, we find the rhino and finish the job.'

'Mutthiji, I think we'll just go home. I'll tell Papa and Mamma they can't send Roly-Poly to the zoo and that I won't go back to boarding school.'

Mutthiji shook his head. 'Once the tarpan has got underway, it cannot be retracted,' he bluffed. 'It must be completed, or a terrible fate will befall the ruling family.'

'We're not the ruling family any more, and anyway, I think that's nonsense!' said Prince Shammy.

'It doesn't matter what you think, huzoor, it must be completed. So come on, get into the Gypsy ... we follow the rhino ... He must have left a trail like a tank.'

'I don't want to shoot Hulla anymore!' the prince said, as Teesta clutched his arm and squeezed it happily. 'He's too magnificent to destroy. It would be like bombing the Taj!'

'You have to! It is your sacred, bounden duty! Or you will be condemning your daduji's spirit to doom—and also your papa!'

'How do you know? How does anyone know?' Both the prince and Teesta asked simultaneously and stared at each other.

'It's ancient knowledge, huzoor. Not to be questioned.'

'It's superstition! Ancient hogwash!'

'Whatever, but it must be completed now.'

'I'm not going to complete it. It will be a sin to kill a rhino like Hulla for some stupid superstition.'

Mutthiji sighed. So it had come to this. Slowly, he raised his rifle and pointed it towards the children. 'You have no choice, huzoor,' he said softly. 'Now cooperate and we'll get this over with quickly.'

'Are you pointing a gun at me, Mutthiji?' the prince asked incredulously.

'Yes, and I will not hesitate to pull the trigger on both of you if you do not do as I say.'

'Very well—I'm sorry to have to do this,' the prince said calmly and lifted his Winchester and fired it point blank at Mutthiji. Again he was flung violently backwards by the recoil, and again nothing happened to Mutthiji, who merely winced and then smiled. It was not a nice smile at all.

'Wha ...?' Teesta shrieked and then ran to the prince, sprawled yet again on the path.

Mutthiji walked up to the children, his gun steady on them.

'Blanks!' he said. 'I loaded your gun with blanks. Come on, get into the Gypsy! We will do this my way now.' One by one he tied their hands behind their backs and then squashed them into the narrow space between the Gypsy's rear seats, making them sit down back to back. Then, he tied their ankles and gagged them. And finally he wound the rope around their chests, tethering the ends to the seat brackets on either side. Teesta faced forwards, glaring at the two front seats and windshield. The prince looked out over the tail light.

'That'll make sure you don't move,' Mutthiji said with grim satisfaction. Then, carefully, he placed the two guns on the rear bench seats: his own on the seat on the right and the prince's on the one on the left.

'This is yours, and that is mine!' he crowed, grinning, pointing them out. 'Remember that, Your Majesty!' The prince glowered at him.

In the rain-softened mud, Hulla had left a pristine set of fresh prints and like many animals in the park, he too preferred using the established paths. They bumped slowly along the track, Mutthiji leaning out of the door and following the tracks. All too soon, it became clear where the big rhino seemed to be going.

'He seems to be heading for Akash bheel,' Mutthiji told the children conversationally. 'Must be going to see Gaindaben.'

Jammed together, back to back, rather like Roly-Poly and Rumble-Tumble had been in the coils of Madame Squeezy, Prince Shammy felt Teesta's cold little fingers wriggling against his. Suddenly he realized that while there was no way they could untie the knots binding their own wrists, they could work on each other's! Which was exactly what Teesta had started doing in real earnest! Mutthiji had foolishly tied their wrists together, leaving their fingers free to move and wiggle. And, because the prince was royalty after all (and old habits of deference die hard), he had tied the prince's wrists relatively loosely. Teesta worked her little fingers madly at the knots around the prince's wrists. She felt him turn his head towards hers, so she too turned hers.

She nodded and he blinked in acknowledgement to let her know he understood what she was doing.

*

In her stable at the SRPG HQ, Roly-Poly thought over the events that had taken place at Hyacinth bheel earlier that day. She had saved Rumble-Tumble from the python, and *his mother* had saved her from the tiger! Which surely meant that she loved her, or at least cared for her a little bit. Which meant, she ought not mind her being Rumble-Tumble's girlfriend. Which meant, she ought to go to Akash bheel right away and be united with him again. She eyed the stable door contemptuously and lowered her head. It shattered on impact and she was out of the house in no time at all. Teesta's mom, fast asleep, thanks to Mutthiji's medication in her dinner, heard nothing. Out in the moon-bathed yard, Roly-Poly sniffed the air. From the paddock, old Bakrasahib trotted over, alarmed.

'What are you doing? Where do you think you are going?' he bleated.

'I'm going to find Rumble-Tumble, and don't you try and stop me!' Roly-Poly tossed her head in the air and trotted down the path. She'd been to Akash bheel so many times before, accompanied by the elephants, that she knew the way blindfolded.

In the meantime, Baghbahadur and Madame Squeezy had retreated into the jungle to nurse their bruised egos as the hyena gang circled them at a safe distance and giggled mockingly at them.

'First, those little piggies stomped on me and then that little rhino chicklet which I had held in my embrace all night!' Madame Squeezy hissed, her eyes blazing. 'The young these days have no respect for their elders and betters.'

Baghbahadur had less reason to feel bad. Being driven away by a furious rhino-mom was no disgrace really—every animal kept out of their way. What irked him was the way the tasty little piglets had squealed with laughter when it had happened.

Roly-Poly arrived safely at Akash bheel twenty minutes after she had escaped from her stable. It looked beautiful: bathed under a silvery full moon, the water pleated platinum and ebony. She trotted down the path slowly, sniffing the air and twitching her cute little ears. A swirl of breeze carried her perfume straight to Rumble-Tumble, dozing at his mother's side, and his scent swirling back to her. Both the little rhinos stiffened. Gaindaben grunted in her sleep and shifted her huge legs.

'Roly-Poly!'

'Rumble-Tumble!'

The two little rhinos regarded each other from either end of the jungle track, squinting furiously. Their ears and noses were telling them beautiful things, their eyes, alas, couldn't quite make out the details. They moved towards each other, slowly at first and then broke into a trot as they drew close. And then they were standing together, nuzzling in the moonlight, making soft goofy snuffling noises at each other.

'Your mom?' Roly-Poly whispered with a giggle.

'She's dozing. Besides, it doesn't matter. She likes you!' Suddenly they froze.

A loud crashing from the northern end of the bheel was accompanied by the wild trashing of grass.

'Oh God, it's that idiot Bhaisaraja and his harem,' Rumble-Tumble said. 'We better get off the path or they'll trample us. They're road hogs!'

'No, look! It's him!' Roly-Poly whispered.

'Papa!' said Rumble-Tumble, sniffing madly.

His huge flanks heaving, Hulla had emerged on the path, sniffing and snorting loudly as he peered myopically down the path.

'It's you lovey-dovey kids again, isn't it?'

'We … we were just talking … about homework,' Rumble-Tumble stuttered.

'I need to see your mother, boy!' Hulla snorted. 'Where is she?'

'May I ask what the hell is going on here?' They whirled around. Gaindaben was standing behind the two little rhinos, tapping one giant foot up and down interrogatively. 'What have you two been doing?'

'Nn… nothing we ought not to, Mamma,' Rumble-Tumble stammered.

'Gaindaben, I have to talk to you,' Hulla said, lumbering towards her.

'You! What are you doing here?' Again, those damn knees of hers were a dead give-away. Not to mention the slight quiver in her voice.

'Th… they shot at me! I nearly died!'

'Who?' Gaindaben was shocked. Hulla had gone right up to her and leant against her, snorting. 'That little pipsqueak prince! Of course, I was charging him at the time, but still, it was most unreasonable. Hey, steady on, you nearly fell over!'

'I'm good!' Gaindaben steadied herself the best she could, breathing rapidly. 'Hey, are you okay? You're trembling! You idiot, if you charged him, of course he's going to shoot! It's called self-defence! You kids, why are you listening to grown-ups talk? Run along and play. I have matters to discuss with your father, Rumble-Tumble.'

Delighted, the two baby rhinos moved off up the path, butting and nudging each other.

'So … so what else do you want to tell me?' Gaindaben asked in a voice fainter than she wished it to be.

'Wh… when I charged towards that fellow holding the gun, knowing he would pull the trigger, I … I could only think of you, Gaindaben,' Hulla whispered. 'But I don't know why. Could you tell me?'

'You don't know why, eh?' Gaindaben didn't know whether to butt Hulla into the bheel or nuzzle him.

'Duh, no, dunno,' he said, staring at her, his mouth puckered up. 'I'm a bit confused!'

'I can see that. Let's go for a moonlight swim, shall we?'

'What about that croc woman?' Hulla asked.

'Her back's gone,' Gaindaben replied.

'The kids?' Hulla inquired.

'They're playing happily. That little one saved my baba's life, so she's okay.'

The two giant rhinos were just about to step into the silvered waters of the bheel when they heard the soft sound of an engine. Its headlights doused, the khaki palace Gypsy had driven onto the path and stopped. Mutthiji stood up in the driver's seat and took in the scene with satisfaction. To one side, and unseen, Roly-Poly and Rumble-Tumble stood stock still and watched.

It had been a bumpy, thumpy ride as Mutthiji followed the trail Hulla had left behind as he plunged through the jungle towards Akash bheel. Teesta continued to work her little fingers tirelessly at the knots binding the prince's wrists. At last she felt the final knot coming undone and dug her elbows into the prince's ribs to let him know. Relieved, Prince Shammy wriggled and extracted one hand, flexing his fingers. But he still couldn't move very much—firmly tethered as they were by the rope that bound them together, anchored to the seat brackets. But at least he could free Teesta's hands, just as she had done his.

But she had turned towards him again and was urgently shaking her head and looking at the Winchester lying on the seat. She turned her head and stared at the second gun and in a flash he understood what she was trying to tell him. He nodded. Oh no, he wasn't thinking of picking up the gun and firing a blind shot at Mutthiji from his awkward position. Firstly, he was facing the wrong way. Secondly, all that movement would alert Mutthiji in no time, and thirdly, he was not going to risk firing off such a powerful rifle in a lurching vehicle with his precious Teesta jammed behind him! Even if he did manage to blow Mutthiji's head off, the vehicle could overturn and catch fire and they were both still tied firmly in place! But there was something else he could do … and that's what Teesta had indicated. Very, very carefully, he reached out with his free hand towards the right rear seat …

Several interminable minutes later, he had completed his task. He felt Teesta turn her face again, her dark eyes glowing. She put her little gagged mouth to his and gave him what had to pass as the first true kiss they had ever exchanged. Prince Shamsher went scarlet but let the kiss linger as long as she wanted. Then they felt the Gypsy slow down. Quickly, he put his hands behind his back again and felt Teesta try to clumsily re-tie his knots in whatever way she could.

*

At the palace, uproar had broken out. Rosy and Posy had sneaked into the prince's bedroom for a late game of cards and had found him missing. The security had been roused and the maharani was freaking out.

'I'm telling you, he's run away with that horrible little village girl he was playing with in the waterhole,' the maharani wailed. 'Now our name will be tarnished. Why did we come back to this godforsaken place! We were so happy in Monte Carlo!'

'Mutthiji has gone too. Shamsher has taken Mutthiji with him, so he's probably all right,' the maharaja said. 'He must be out having a night in the jungle, hunting and shooting and boozing—like a man! I told you boarding school was good for him!'

It was the prince's dadiji, who everyone was ignoring now as they yelled at each other, who discovered the missing Winchesters in the gun cabinet. She went a bit pale and then got on her phone.

'Commander Thapa? This is Rajmataji ...'

Out in the southern ranges of the park, searching in vain for non-existent poachers, Commander Thapa listened as Rajmata explained what had happened and what she feared was about to take place.

'Very well, Rajmataji, we shall spread out and search. Hulla's guard has reported that he is not at the Hyacinth bheel—he seems to have lost him. He had to leave Hulla for a while because of some hoax emergency. Someone had called him and told him that a rhino had fallen into another trap nearby, and he went to check. When he got back, Hulla was gone.'

'If you are passing this way, will you pick me up?' the prince's dadiji requested. 'The maharaja doesn't seem to be very bothered, and the maharani thinks Shamsher has run away with a village girl!'

'Yes, Rajmataji, we shall pick you up! We should be there in half an hour.'

*

'Come on, get out!' Mutthiji opened the tailgate and clambered in to release the children. He was in a hurry now—he wanted to get this plan (that had already gone off the rails) over with as quickly as possible. He didn't realize that the prince's wrists came free quicker than they should have. He untied their feet and they stumbled out of the Gypsy, rubbing their chafed wrists and ankles. He handed the prince the Winchester that had been lying on the seat on the left.

'Your gun, sire. Now go and shoot that fellow,' he said with an insane giggle, pointing towards Hulla at the edge of the bheel. 'With a blank cartridge. It should be interesting.' He paused. 'If you refuse, I will shoot off the ear of your little friend,' he went on, jabbing the rifle's barrel at Teesta. 'First one ear, then the next—they bleed horribly. And then, maybe shoot off her nose and hands and feet and stomach. So get on with it, boy!'

'You dare call me "boy"? You'll never get away with this, Mutthiji!'

'Oh yes, I will.'

'You're mad, Mutthiji! What are you going to get out of this?'

Mutthiji told him, gloating, 'The whole kingdom of Gaindagunj and its vast treasury, Your Highness! Go on now. Don't waste any more time!'

'I want to be at the prince's side when he shoots Hulla,' Teesta said unexpectedly. Mutthiji shrugged.

'Very well, no problem … you can both be trampled and gored side by side. Just like a Bollywood film, no?'

He jabbed the gun in their direction. Slowly Prince Shammy and Teesta walked together down the track leading towards the water, where, just at the edge, they could see the enormous bulks of Hulla and Gaindaben.

'Shoot him now!' Mutthiji exhorted. The two huge rhinos whirled around, sloshing the muddy water, as they heard his voice.

Teesta put her lips to the prince's ear. 'You better shoot Mutthiji now,' she whispered. 'What are you waiting for?'

The prince grinned. 'I have a better idea,' he said. 'Come on, let's go back.'

'Boy, Your Highness, what are you doing?' Mutthiji squawked as the children turned around and began walking towards him. Behind them the two short-sighted rhinos snorted and sniffed the air suspiciously. On the path to one side of the Gypsy, Roly-Poly and Rumble-Tumble remained still as statues, watching.

'Mutthiji, I swapped the rifles,' said Prince Shammy conversationally. 'You've picked up the wrong one. You placed your Winchester on the right hand seat and mine on the left, and told me to remember it. So I did, and swapped them. So, fire away!' He paused. 'But if I do ...'

'Wha... what?' Mutthiji stared suspiciously at his rifle. 'Nonsense—you couldn't have done that!' Suddenly, his face went hard. He lifted the Winchester and aimed it at the children.

'Hey!' Teesta suddenly went very pale. 'Are you sure you swapped the rifles, Shammy?' she asked, a dreadful doubt assailing her.

'I did,' he whispered back, cool as you please. 'He's got the dud. Only I can't really fire this—it kicks like a mule. You saw what happened last time—it nearly knocked me out! My shoulder's already terribly sore.'

But Mutthiji could fire—and he did. The flash and blast sent sleeping birds skittering into the sky and Hulla straight into Gaindaben.

'See! I told you!' he hollered, panic-stricken. 'Let's get out of here!'

'The babies!' Gaindaben shrieked, pushing Hulla off her and beginning to charge. She was too late.

Roly-Poly had beaten her to it. 'That fellow shot at them!' She put her little head down and hit Mutthiji amidships, sending him flying.

'That'll teach you!' she snorted, as Rumble-Tumble joined her, snorting, and doing stylish handbrake turns. Mutthiji lay gasping in the mud, the breath knocked out of him. When he opened his eyes, he found the prince standing over him with the Winchester.

'Now you know! So get up!'

'Roly-Poly,' Teesta squealed as she flung her arms around her little rhino. 'You rescued us again!'

Gaindaben too had halted her charge and was rear-ended by Hulla.

'Oof! Sorry, my dear,' he snorted. 'You stopped without warning. But what's going on?'

And then, Maharani and Hira trumpeted as they stepped out of the grass with Commander Thapa, Jawahar Singh, Rajmataji, Rosy and Posy (who had absolutely insisted on coming along for this biggest adventure of their lives and had filmed everything) and several guards on their backs. They had arrived some minutes earlier and had witnessed everything, too shocked and afraid to interfere, lest it provoked a charge from the rhinos or made Mutthiji shoot the children.

The two giant rhinos stood side by side, heaving and snorting uncertainly. Teesta had her arms around Roly-Poly, while Rumble-Tumble retreated nervously and then went and stood by his parents. Prince Shammy stood next to Teesta, staring in relief at the elephants. Mutthiji staggered to his feet, gasping and wheezing, and found himself looking down the barrels of half a dozen guns. Quietly, he raised his hands. Then Teesta released Roly-Poly and whispered to her, 'Go to Gaindaben—she won't harm you, baby. I'm here.'

Roly-Poly snuffled and trotted off towards Gaindaben who grunted and then butted her gently.

'I think ...' Gaindaben said faintly, turning to Hulla, 'I think we need to see Gau Mataji right away. This is all becoming too much for me. My nerves are shot!'

Prince Shammy turned to Teesta. 'Come on,' he said, 'let's go home now!'

Epilogue

'What?' the maharaja roared. 'You tried to perform the tarpan?'

'With a rifle that fired blanks!' the maharani shrieked. 'Are you out of your mind?'

Rajmata stepped forward. 'If anyone is to blame, it is me,' she said. 'I told him stories of the great tarpan hunts of the past every time he came home and he loved it. Of course, I didn't know he was going to try it by himself with the help of that villainous Mutthi!' She then looked at Prince Shammy fondly. 'He is a very brave young man and is fortunate to have found an even braver little friend. They need not have to prove anything more to the world ever again.'

The brave young man and his braver little friend stood in front of the outraged royal parents and took their medicine. Teesta knew that she was going to get another dose of it from her father, who had been acutely embarrassed.

'Yes,' the prince mumbled, 'I wanted to, and then Mutthiji said I had to, but I didn't know the rifle had blanks. Teesta saved my life.' Of course, he wasn't about to tell his parents why he did it.

'You let a little ragamuffin girl save your life?' the maharani shrieked and emptied her glass of pink gin.

'And you saw what Roly-Poly did! She saved us both from Mutthiji!' the prince responded. He went on bitterly, '… And you want to send her to a zoo!'

'You are not going back to boarding school—that's final!' the maharaja roared. 'That's where you picked up all these hare-brained ideas, I'm sure. You will go to the local school here, where … where someone can keep an eye on you … and drill some sense into you.'

'He can attend the Gaindaganj National Park High School that I go to,' Teesta piped up innocently. 'We can both go on Hira and I can keep an eye on him.' The maharani helped herself to yet another large pink gin (her third) and peered owlishly at Teesta.

'I can't quite make out who you are, darling,' she said. 'That horrible little ragamuffin who Shamsher was disporting with in the waterhole with that rhino, or

Commander Thapa's pretty little daughter? You look like both of them!'

'Doesn't matter, ma'am,' said Teesta, dropping a curtsy.

'Mamma, that little rhino saved both our lives. Mutthiji would have shot us to smithereens otherwise. You can't send her away to a zoo!'

The maharani shuddered. 'Who says she's going to be sent to a zoo? She'll just cause havoc there—charging at all the keepers and breaking out and running amok in Gaindagunj town. I heard how she escaped from her stable. She can roam here—maybe that big old cow rhino can teach her some manners.'

'Can we go now, please?' the prince asked his parents.

'Run along. We have to leave for the airport in ten minutes. Be good and don't get into any more trouble.'

The two children walked out of the grand Durbar hall. Out on the broad, breezy verandah, Teesta and Prince Shammy exchanged glances, their eyes shining. They walked down the grand stairway. In the courtyard, Maharani stood, waiting patiently. Commander Thapa had accompanied Teesta and was, in fact, now interrogating Mutthiji in the palace's basement cells. It seemed he had been responsible for the poaching incidents as well. Teesta looked at the prince.

'Elephant ride?' she suggested, her eyes bright.

'Sure! Where should we go?'

'I know where …'

A little while later, they regarded each other comfortably from their wallows in the Chhoti Talao.

'See, I told you it would work!' the prince said loftily. 'I don't have to go back to boarding school and Roly-Poly doesn't have to go to the zoo.'

'Yes,' Teesta said. 'And you were ready to shoot poor old Hulla for that.'

'Nah!' he said airily. 'I knew my rifle had blanks. I couldn't kill old Hulla!'

'Liar! You fired at him.'

'Only to scare him. I knew there was no bullet in the gun …' But he was going red.

'Liar, liar, pants on fire!'

'Um … well, ya, I only really knew after I had fired.' He grinned sheepishly and swallowed. 'Th … thanks for rescuing me,' he went on, squeezing her little hand. 'I thought we were done for! That gun has the kick of a mule. Why did you?'

'Why did I what?'

'Rescue me? You could have stayed up in the tree!'

'And watched Hulla make halva of you? Ew! I thought you'd gone nuts. And I didn't want you to shoot him.'

'Thanks again!'

'No problem,' she said, grinning. 'You know what I think is the best part? Old Gaindaben has made friends with Roly-Poly. So now she can teach her the ways of a wild rhino.' She paused and gulped. 'Better than I ever could,' she went on sadly.

'Well, you're almost a rhino. You sure charged at me like a little rhino!' he said, grinning.

'What?' She turned towards him, her eyes flashing. 'I am not!' She lowered her head. 'But let me show you. I can do a pretty good imitation!'

OTHER BOOKS BY RANJIT LAL